SPRINGFIRE

Also by Terie Garrison

AutumnQuest
WinterMaejic

Forthcoming by Terie Garrison

SummerDanse

SPRINGFIRE

TERIE GARRISON

Woodbury, Minnesota

First Edition
First Printing, 2007

Book design by Steffani Sawyer
Cover design by Gavin Dayton Duffy
Cover image © 2007 BrandX
Editing by Rhiannon Ross

Flux, an imprint of Llewellyn Publications

Library of Congress Cataloging-in-Publication Data
The Cataloging-in-Publication Data for *SpringFire* is on file at the Library of Congress.
   ISBN-13: 978-0-7387-1096-9
   ISBN-10: 0-7387-1096-2

Flux
A Division of Llewellyn Worldwide, Ltd.
2143 Wooddale Drive, Dept. 0738710962
Woodbury, MN 55125-2989, U.S.A.
www.fluxnow.com

Printed in the United States of America

To Sally

Acknowledgements

Special thanks to Marion Engelke,
host of many of the words.

And to Elizabeth Moon and George Dzuik,
for help with Things I Don't Know Much About.

And to the South Manchester Writers' Workshop.
Of course.

The Candles

Week 1	Peace	Ivory	Ginger
Week 2	Honesty	Pink	Sweet Pea
Week 3	Resourcefulness	Blue	Rosemary
Week 4	Strength	Forest Green	Sage
Week 5	Clarity	Lavender	Thyme
Week 6	Health	Pale Green	Melon
Week 7	Diligence	White	Carnation
Week 8	Creativity	Orange	Orange
Week 9	Generosity	Purple	Lavender
Week 10	Kindness	Yellow	Lemon
Week 11	Humility	Turquoise	Berry
Week 12	Love	Red	Cinnamon

The Candlesticks

Autumn	Water	Silver
Winter	Earth	Copper
Spring	Air	Crystal
Summer	Fire	Gold

-from The Book of Lore

A half-played game of Talisman and Queen lies before me, the jewel pieces glowing as they sit on the black velvet, embroidered with glittering silver thread. The Queen's Heart, made of ruby, gleams at the center. Ranged about are the Talismans: mine, emerald; my opponent's, sapphire.

I cannot see against whom I play. Shrouded in shadow, the brooding presence sits, absorbing energy and my concentration. It seems to suck the very air from the room. I can scarce breathe.

The game is almost won. My heart tells me that with a single move, I will Secure the Queen's Heart. But my brain is frozen, unable to make sense of the game pieces. A wrong move, and my enemy will take all.

A voice breaks the silence—a familiar male voice that echoes around the room growing in power instead of fading away.

"Your move," it says.

And everything goes dark. All I can see is the fine silver lines against a black world.

"Your move," the voice says again, taking the last of the air with it.

I fall into a black pit of nothingness.

And then I awake.

One

Watching the antics of twenty-three baby dragons, I couldn't help laughing. They'd been born—not hatched—a month ago, and I still wasn't used to all the silly things they did.

Like clambering up a tree trunk and crowing superiority over the others, only to discover that it was a long, frightening way down to the ground. They could all fly, the gossamer of their red wings looking transparent and pink against the Winter sky, but they still often forgot about this ability in the heat of their play battles.

Or like chasing each other around the cave, their chirps and squeals rising in volume until it drove us humans out into the chilly, early Spring air to save our hearing.

Or like now, when they gathered in their wallow inside the cave, writhing and intertwining themselves in some strange form of "tag," with Xyla, their mother, watching indulgently.

As I watched the huge puddle of dragons rippling, I tried to figure out the game. The head of one of the babies rose above the other and let out a triumphant creel, only to have its face swatted by two tails. It sank back into the swirling, heaving mass.

"Guess that one didn't win this time, eh, Donavah?" I

jumped at Grey's voice next to me. "Have you sorted out exactly what they're doing?"

As it always did these days, my heart beat a little faster whenever he was near me. Keeping my eyes on the dragons, I shook my head. Then, with exquisitely bad timing, I yawned.

Grey put a hand on my arm. "Did you have that dream again last night?"

I felt my face go hot. The recurring dream I'd been having every night for the past week was *not* what I wanted to talk to Grey about. I composed my face into a smile and looked up at him, to find his handsome grey eyes, after which he'd been named, boring into mine.

"Yes, same dream. But not so bad this time." I hoped he'd believe the lie.

Chase, Grey's white and brown hound, darted up just then and shoved his nose under my hand. When I scratched his head, his tail wagged and his body wriggled in pure doggy pleasure.

The dog's raspy voice spoke in my head. "I know I can always rely on you. Oh, and it's quite easy to see what they're doing."

"Really?" I asked. "And are you going to enlighten me?"

"No. Figure it out yourself!" And with that, he raced off.

Grey chuckled, and I wondered whether Chase had spoken to both of us or only to me. Animals could communicate their thoughts with mages, and could even choose whether to speak only to one or to several.

"He certainly likes you," Grey said.

"The feeling's mutual."

Then I thought of something. "Did Chase tell you I had that dream? He's always right there next to me when I wake up." It would be just like the dog to tell Grey something was bothering me. From our very first meeting, Chase had always looked after me.

The corners of Grey's mouth twitched. "Well, to tell the truth, he did. He knows I worry about you."

I looked quickly away, not wanting him to see the blush that crept up my face again. Grey worried about me? Not exactly the feeling I would've chosen, but it was better than nothing.

"Do you have any idea why you keep having that particular dream?"

Speaking carefully so that I would sound as normal as possible, I said, "No. I don't even play Talisman and Queen. But," I shuddered, "it's that voice that's so disturbing. I wake up terrified, as if something very wrong will happen if I don't make the right move."

Grey sighed. "I wish I could make it stop."

"Me, too," I said, then pressed my lips together. I often fell asleep imagining ways Grey could stop the dreams.

An awkward silence fell between us, which Grey broke by clapping his hands together once in a business-like fashion and saying, "Well, I'd better get going. It takes most of the day to keep this lot fed." He shook his head. "I can't imagine how you all would've gotten by without me this past week. Somehow, I just don't see Yallick and Oleeda as the hunting types."

This was very true. As mages, they could hunt quite skillfully when it was necessary. But it would've taken both of them together all day to catch what Grey did in just a few hours. I guessed it was the difference between being a young man brought up as a hunter and being an old mage.

I looked back at the baby dragons. "Everyone is really glad you came." I managed not to add, "Especially me."

"Not everyone," Grey said with a snort. "Yallick wishes I was far, far away. If not dead."

I allowed myself a sidelong glance at him. "That's not true. Why should he care? And you've been so helpful with the baby dragons."

"I don't know why he cares, but he makes it clear with every frown that I'm not welcome."

"Oh, that doesn't mean anything. He just likes acting cross." Which wasn't strictly true, but in the few months I'd been his apprentice, I'd learned not to take his scowls and severe looks very seriously.

A high-pitched shriek echoed around the cave, and Xyla finally put an end to the game with an even louder trumpet. The red pile of baby dragons swiftly turned into a river streaming out of the cave.

Xyla turned her giant head toward me and Grey. "I will help with the hunt," she said, her voice in my head clear, strong, and musical. "Grey has been helpful, but I must do my share of the work."

"Xyla says she'll help with the hunt," I told Grey. He was already smiling.

"If we can fly, there's a meadow about ten miles from here where there's a huge herd of elk. With Xyla's help, we could bring back enough food to feed the babies *and* the whole camp."

Xyla went out and, once free of the confines of the cave, she stretched her huge wings. It was a clear cold day, and the sun made her red hide glow like a jewel. A jewel the size of a house.

"So, um, coming with?" Grey asked.

My breath caught in my throat. I couldn't help but grin. For more than one reason. I loved flying on Xyla more than almost anything in the world, but any excuse to spend more time alone with Grey was also welcome.

By the time I'd put on my heavy cloak, gloves, and boots, Grey had gathered his hunting gear and put on his own cloak. Xyla stood in the clearing in front of the cave, watching her scattered brood as they slithered in and out, up and down the trees beyond.

Traz came running up. "Hey, can I go, too?"

I sighed. I'd hoped to be alone with Grey, but how could I say no to Traz? He was only ten, but we'd become fast friends when he helped me rescue my brother, Breyard, from sure execution. He wasn't maejic, so he couldn't speak to or hear the dragons, but he loved Xyla and her babies.

Grey spoke before I did. "Someone needs to stay here and tell Yallick where we've gone when he gets back."

My heart gave a little flutter. So Grey didn't want company, either.

Traz glared at Grey.

"I have told Yallick that we are going hunting," Xyla told me.

Traz forced a pathetic, puppy-dog-lost look into his eyes, one he knew I couldn't resist.

"All right, you can come. Hurry up and get your riding gear."

He dashed to the cave.

"I was hoping we'd be able to have that talk we've been trying to have," Grey said, almost under his breath.

"I know, but I really have a hard time saying no to him, especially when Xyla wants him to come." I gave her leg a fond pat. "Besides, would you want to have to spend the afternoon with Yallick if you were only ten?"

Grey let out a snort. "I'm more than twice ten, and I wouldn't want to."

Ignoring the reminder that at twenty-one he was nearly six years older than me, I just said, "I better get my pack. Then I can have something hot ready for you to drink after you've finished hunting."

I trotted back to the cave, passing Traz on his way out, twirling his staff while his heavy jacket flapped open.

"Close that up properly," I said.

"Yes, Mother."

I shook my head and kept going. My pack lay near my sleeping pallet. I checked it to make sure I had everything I needed, throwing in an extra pair of woolly socks; it might get cold sitting around while Xyla and Grey hunted.

When I returned to the others, Traz was, as usual, brandishing his staff as he practiced moves he was learning in his martial arts lessons.

Grey had a sour look on his face and wasn't playing along. "You're going to poke someone's eye out with that thing," he grumbled.

"Ha!" Traz shouted. "No, I won't. I have much better control than that." He held it vertically, spun round, and brought it down a fraction of an inch from my nose as I jerked to a stop.

"Traz!" I cried. "Grey's right. You're going to hurt someone." His wide grin fell at my sharp tone.

"But I didn't," he protested. "I knew exactly where to stop so I wouldn't hurt you."

"And what if I hadn't stopped walking? You might've broken my nose."

Traz pulled the staff away from my face and rubbed his hand along its smooth, shiny surface.

"Oh, it's all right. I'm not mad. Just try to be a little more careful when you're not actually training, all right? Now let's go. Those babies aren't getting any less hungry while we stand around talking."

Xyla let out another call, and the babies all streamed back into the cave.

Yallick appeared on the path out of the woods and walked over to us. The mages had spent the morning meeting at one of the other caves—one where it was quiet—and he must have returned when Xyla told him we were leaving.

"Hunt well," he said in his gravelly voice, giving Traz a boost up the dragon's side.

"You might want to get a pit ready so we can roast an elk," said Grey. "Everyone will eat well tonight."

Yallick actually smiled at Grey, his bright blue-green eyes lighting up at the suggestion of a feast. "I will do that. Just bring my young charges back safely."

"That I will, sir," Grey said with a quick nod.

By this time, I'd shouldered my pack. Traz reached his

staff down to help me. I grabbed it, scrambled up, and took my usual place behind him. We'd traveled like this many times on our journey in the Autumn, and it felt like the good old days to be at it again. A moment later, Grey sat behind me, his arms lightly encircling my waist. So lightly they might as well not have been there at all.

Then Xyla rose into the air. I looked down at Yallick to see him waving at us with one hand while the other smoothed his long, white-blond hair away from his face.

From this height, I could see how the mountainside was pockmarked with caves. There were more than fifty mages living here in hiding from the Royal Guard. For having mae-jic—a higher form of magic—was a capital offence in this land of Alloway, and King Erno was determined to wipe it out once and for all.

We soared through the air, the wind blowing my hair back and practically freezing the tip of my nose. But the glory of the flight made that worthwhile. Trees stretched for miles. The mountain ridges cut a sharp, jagged line against the bright morning sky. The life vibrations of the forest, both the trees and all the creatures living in it, swelled my heart and filled me with wonder. Life, in all its forms, tasted sweet.

Xyla swept around to the left and circled high over a meadow below, where a dark smudge must be the herd Grey had mentioned.

The dragon began to descend at a gentle angle, and as she did, the meadow grew rapidly in size. She landed on the opposite side from where the elk were so as not to frighten them into taking cover too soon.

Grey immediately walked off toward the herd. He would kill as many as possible before they even realized an intruder was among them. Then Xyla would join the hunt.

In the meantime, I started a small fire on the edge of the meadow near a long-fallen, rotting log. It was the easiest time I'd ever had lighting a fire. The thick trees overhead had kept the rotting wood relatively dry, and it flared into flame with the first spark. Traz took the staff a short distance away and started practicing his moves again.

Half an hour later, I heard the thudding roar of hooves—hundreds of them—in the distance, making the ground shake. Xyla took wing then and began picking beasts from the herd while chasing them back toward Grey. With Xyla helping, I knew the hunt would be fast and I needn't worry about getting trampled with her watching out for me.

Grey would be back soon now, so I took my saucepan and waterskin from my pack and began heating the water.

When he arrived, I handed him a tin cup full of steaming tea. He wrapped his bare fingers around it, smiling appreciatively. Traz added a little more sweetening to his own cup, while I poured the last of the tea into mine. We stood around the fire in silence, sipping our hot drinks and moving around a little whenever the wind changed direction and blew smoke into someone's eyes.

"Ten elk," Grey finally said. "Not a bad hour's work."

Traz gaped at him. "Ten elk? In that short time?"

Grey grinned. "It helps to have a dragon helping out. I only brought down four of them myself."

"*Only* four?" Traz squeaked. "When are you going to start teaching me to shoot?"

"As soon as … " Grey's voice trailed off.

"As soon as he's taught *me*," I said.

"Not fair! I'll be ancient by then!"

We all laughed. It was the first time we'd acted as if we were all friends, and it felt nice. Very nice.

We kicked the fire out and made sure all the embers were dead, then Traz and I climbed onto Xyla's back. Grey had rigged a rope sling that allowed Xyla to carry a number of the elk at a time, but it still would take two trips.

As we tried to get the ropes in place, a sense of darkness washed over me. My mood plunged into deepest gloom, and, as if it were being whispered straight into my ear, a voice said, "Your move."

A shudder shook my frame. Traz looked back at me as the voice said it again. "Your move."

I couldn't breathe. Blackness started closing in on my sight.

Xyla threw her head up in alarm and let out an ear-piercing scream. The blackness disappeared, replaced with a feeling of dread. Grey took one look at the dragon and a split-second later was rushing toward us. With a great leap, he was halfway up her back and he'd barely got in place behind me when she sprang into the air.

My heart thudded in my chest as I tried to force air into my lungs. I lost my balance and began to slip off as the ground receded faster than ever before.

"They come!" Xyla's voice shrieked inside my head. Her

panic completely overwhelmed me, and I couldn't tell how much of my fear was hers and how much my own. I scarcely realized that Grey was holding tightly onto me.

"My babies!" Xyla's vocal cries deafened my ears and her mental cries froze my mind.

We streaked through the air back to the cave-pocked mountainside where the mages were hidden. But before we got there, red and green lightning shot up from the ground and across the sky.

"No, Xyla!" I couldn't tell if I shouted the words aloud or only in my mind. "We can't go there! It's the dragonmasters!"

But she didn't listen. Or couldn't hear. We plummeted toward the earth. Then the lightning was all around us. It would strike any moment and kill us all.

With a sudden sheer almost straight up, Xyla screamed again. I was sure she'd been hit. A flash in front of us blinded me. A sizzle shot past my head, and the energy of it seized my thoughts. A last jerk, and then we were falling. My heart squeezed in my chest, and I knew no more.

✦

The reflection of the world sparkles in the window of time.

Gazing upon one another, smiling or storming or dancing or raging as the mood take them, the parallel worlds float upon the ether.

A life passes between them on a thread, rainbow stars billowing out behind in its wake. And on the return journey, it skews in on itself to end where it began.

Look upon the worlds. See how they glitter with life and blush golden with love.

Let all who understand grow in wisdom.

~*from* The Esoterica of Mysteries

two

When I awoke, the earth spun beneath me. I lay curled up in a ball and shivering a little in the cool air. After a moment, the memory of everything that had happened came flooding back. The Royal Guard. And dragonmasters! They must have captured us, and I must be in a cell somewhere. And that meant that they had Xyla, too. Again. They'd captured her once before to force her to fight in the king's pits. Futility overwhelmed me.

And they'd have all the babies, too!

With a groan of despair, I sat up to find that I was back in the clearing in front of the cave. Traz and Grey both lay nearby, still asleep or unconscious, I wasn't sure which, and Xyla, too, sprawled on the ground. More like a dead thing.

Stiff as I was, I got to my feet and tottered over to her. She was breathing, but shallowly, as if it were hard to draw breath. Her legs twitched a bit, and her color was off. She was usually a rich, bright red, but now she looked coppery, as if someone had rubbed her with a yellow paste to dull her hide.

She lay on her side, her head on the ground and mouth slightly open. I reached up and touched her face. Her skin felt much cooler than usual, and that was saying a lot, since, as a reptile, she had cold blood.

At my touch, she stirred slightly, and I thought she might

awaken, but she didn't. Instead, her body seemed to wilt, if that were possible. The twitching stopped. I bit my lip, fearing the worst, but no, she took another shallow, shuddering breath. I felt her heartbeat, slow—very slow—but steady.

Then a soft rustling sound behind me. I whirled round to face the menace, only to find Traz sitting up and rubbing his eyes. He let out a small groan, much as I had done, and that seemed to awaken Grey, who also started to stir.

But where was everyone else? Yallick, Oleeda, and the other mages? The dragonmasters? Surely none of them would've just left us all lying here—the former because they were our friends, and the latter because they were our enemies.

"Wha—what happened?" Traz asked in a tremulous voice. "Where are we?"

"I don't know," I said softly, looking around and beginning to wonder if it were a trap.

Grey seemed to have gotten his bearings and rose to his feet, his movements lithe and wary as a hunting cat. I fancied his ears pricked.

I opened my own senses. Usually very sensitive to the life vibrations all around me—so much so that I usually had to block them out—I could feel scarcely anything. Almost as if everything were a quarter-beat out of sync. As long as I didn't concentrate on it, everything was fine, but when I tried to get into rhythm, it made me dizzy; I lost my balance and almost fell, even though I was standing still.

Grey seemed to stagger slightly, too, as he circled the edge of the small clearing. Our eyes locked for a moment and he shook his head. "Nothing," he mouthed.

"Where's Yallick and everyone?" Traz's voice crackled through the still air.

"Shh!" Grey and I both hissed.

Traz got to his feet and came to stand by Xyla and me. "What's wrong with her?" he asked in a hushed whisper as he stroked her neck. He seemed finally to have caught on to our danger.

"I don't know," I answered.

Grey joined us, a knife in each hand. "I wish Chase were here," he said. "I feel half-naked without my dog." He looked around again. "Let's go look in the cave. But carefully, quietly. And let me go first."

Traz glared at Grey's back but followed. I fell in behind him as we crept toward the cave, nerves on edge to catch any sense of disruption. But nothing beyond the soft soughing of the wind in the trees.

The cave mouth was huge, more like a gaping hole in the mountainside, and the cavern beyond was enormous—big enough to house Xyla and her brood of twenty-three, plus more than enough room for several people to live, too.

Of course, the light from the opening didn't shine far into that gigantic space. But it was still enough that we should've been able to see the place where we had our fire. And the ground should've been trampled down; people had been living there, after all, for several months. Instead, the ground just inside was deep with a layer of Autumn leaves blown in by Winter storms. The cave had a distinct air of disuse.

Grey took a few steps inside. "It's no use," he said, coming back out. "I need some light."

"Oh! Of course!" I exclaimed. I unslung my pack and dug out my kit of meditation candles. "These ought to help."

We lit three and each took one. We'd lost the edge of our caution; surely, if anyone were watching and wanted to grab us, they would've done so already.

Going back into the cave, we stayed together to pool the light. Once we were well inside, our eyes began to adjust to the darkness. We couldn't see all the way across, but after one circuit, one thing was very clear: no one had been living here for many years. If ever.

+ + +

It was when we got back outside that something else dawned on me. There was no snow on the ground. How had I missed that before? It just couldn't be. Although it was Spring, we'd recently had a late snowfall and the snow had been deep, except in the clearing and along the paths, where the passing to and fro of people all day every day had tramped it down.

And now there was no sign of anyone anywhere. Not even the paths remained.

Grey and Traz gathered firewood, while I returned to Xyla to check on her. She hadn't stirred, but I could see her eyes moving under her lids as if she were having an agitated dream. I draped my arms around her, trying to coax some kind of response.

By the time the others had gathered enough wood for the afternoon and night, and had gotten a fire roaring inside the cave, I'd grown cold and a little desperate to wake the dragon.

"Xyla," I called, using both my voice and my spirit to try to reach her. "Xyla, you must wake up." It became a chant, and about the twentieth time I said this, her tail twitched. "Xyla!" I cried, putting as much passion into my tone as I could. "Xyla!"

An eyelid fluttered open. An ear flicked.

"Donavah." Her voice inside my head was so weak that I almost didn't catch it.

"Xyla, dear. I'm here. Let's go into the cave. It'll be warmer there."

"Donavah? Warm?"

"Come, my love."

"So tired."

"I know. But please. Get up. The cave is only a few steps away."

She lifted her head a little. "I do not know if I can make it."

"You can. I know you can. I will give you my strength." As if that would help.

But my feeling of urgency must have penetrated her lethargy, because she began to rise. Once she was on her feet, I kept a hand on her leg. Her head drooped pathetically, and I feared she wouldn't make it. We'd awakened around midday, but the sun had long fallen from noon, and the temperature had already begun to drop. She *must* get inside.

She halted and began to sag to the ground again. "No! Xyla, no. Just a little farther. You must keep going."

Grey and Traz came out, and as if they understood the need for skin-to-skin contact, they each took a spot by another of her giant legs. She took a step, then another. A pause, then another.

Finally, after what seemed an eternity, she entered the cave and sank back to the ground. The tip of her tail was still out-side, but we dragged it in and hoped it would be far enough.

I felt overcome with weakness and wondered whether Xyla really had used whatever strength I'd been able to lend her to make that short journey. Then I laughed at myself. Whether she had or not didn't really matter. The simple fact was that I was hungry. How long had it been since I'd last eaten? Hours? Days? Years? *Centuries?*

I sat next to the fire, unable to get to my feet, even though I knew I should. Watching me, Grey scowled. He looked as tired as I felt, but he suddenly dashed outside. I just watched him go. He stalked all around the clearing in front of the cave, looking for something.

Then he let out a disgusted curse and came back inside. "My bow! It's gone!"

"What—" I started, but he interrupted.

"I remember now, I dropped it when I leapt onto Xyla's back. At the meadow," he sighed. "Supper might be small tonight."

"Wait!" Traz said with a note of triumph in his voice. He rummaged around in his pack. "Ha! Got it!" He drew something out from the very bottom and brandished it in the firelight. "My slingshot. Guess supper's on me tonight, O great hunter."

Grey looked at him with eyes narrowed. "Fine," he said with the barest hint of a smile. "Go ahead. I don't mind."

+ + +

After Traz had gone, I found a little dried fruit in my pack and shared it with Grey as we stared into the fire.

Then Grey spoke first.

"I've been thinking about what you told me, about maejic." The night after Xyla's babies were born, I'd explained it to him, how the group I was with were mages—people who had the ancient gift of maejic, a power stronger and older than magic—and that King Erno had set out to destroy the community in an effort to wipe maejic out. I'd told Grey that I had this power, and that when he'd rescued me, I'd been trapped and left to die by Anazian, a mage who had turned against the others.

He'd listened without saying a word, and I'd been so afraid that he would pack up his things and leave. After all, King Erno had made maejic a capital crime. But once I'd finished and he'd had time to absorb it all, all he said was, "So you can hear and speak to Chase?"

"Yes. Well, not during that time at your cabin. Anazian had put a spell on me so that I couldn't use my maejic." I winced a little at the memory of those long days when I'd been bereft of my gift and thought I'd lost it forever. "But the spell was eventually broken." I hadn't told him that Yallick and Oleeda tried to break it and couldn't, and that in the end, I'd somehow—I didn't know how—reached deep within my soul to break it myself. That was still too confusing for me to make any sense out of it.

Now Grey went on. "Well, remember what I told you back when we first met, that my parents abandoned me because something was wrong with me?" I nodded. He took a deep breath. "Well, I'm maejic, too."

A stab of excitement made me sit up even straighter, almost made me leap to my feet. "You're joking! Why haven't you said so before?" I stood up and started pacing back and forth in agitation. "But then, that explains so many things. Like how you always know what the dragons need. And—" understanding dawned on me "—back at your cabin. Chase told you how I was feeling and when I needed anything!" How had I not guessed before now?

Grey picked at his fingernails. "Well, not all the time," he muttered. "Only when it was important. I wasn't spying on you or anything."

"I didn't mean—" I stopped pacing and sat back down next to him. "Grey, this is great! I had no idea. How could I? But why didn't you tell me before?"

He looked at me, his grey eyes piercing me. "How?" Grey's eyes slid from mine. "I don't know. I guess it's just—" He let out a long sigh. "Well, I've always had to hide it from everyone except Malk." He was the hermit who'd raised Grey after his parents abandoned him. "I guess I got into the habit, one that was hard to break."

I understood that. I wanted to reach out and touch him, let him know that it was all right, but I couldn't seem to figure out how to say the words without sounding stupid.

A silence grew between us. Grey eventually broke it. "None of that really matters now anyway. We need to figure out what's going on. The last thing I remember is falling." He shuddered.

"Me, too. I think we got hit by that lightning.

"What was all that, anyway? Do you know?"

The word came out as a whisper. "Dragonmasters." It was my turn to shudder.

"Who are they?"

"They're awful. They're very powerful magicians who work for the king. They wear these black robes, and they move about as if they own the world. And the power just reeks off them. They attacked the mages a few times. That's why we had to go into hiding. And," I lowered my voice, "Xyla herself is afraid of them."

He raised his eyebrows and looked over at her. "That's saying something."

"But how did they find our hiding place in the mountains?" I wondered aloud. "And how did they know Xyla was there? That shows how powerful they are, don't you think?"

Grey turned his attention back to me. "All right, so they attacked, and as you said, some of their lightning must have hit us. Did it—I don't know—move us backward in time or something?"

That took me aback. "Why do you say that?"

Grey let out an exasperated sigh. "Because it's pretty obvious that no one's been here for ages. It's the same place—there's the shelf of rock where all the cooking gear was kept, and the natural chimney is right here," he pointed at the ceiling over the fire, "the same as before."

"I don't know. Is moving in time even possible?"

"I wouldn't have thought so, but I can't think of anything else. It doesn't seem any more likely that we just all lay there unconscious for a few years. If your old dragonmasters had just left us and we didn't wake up, we would've died."

Just then, Xyla let out a groan that echoed around the

cavern, making it sound even louder. I sprang to my feet and rushed to her.

"Xyla, are you all right?" I reached out and placed a hand on her jaw.

"Donavah? You are really here? I am not dreaming?"

That sounded so human I almost laughed. "No, Xyla, you're not dreaming. I'm here. So's Grey. And Traz. Wherever here is."

"You do not know where we are?"

"Well, we're in the cave. But everyone else is gone. We don't know where to."

She let out a long, slow breath that whistled past her nostrils and blew my hair away from my face. "You have not guessed?"

"Guessed what?" Now I was growing a little impatient with her.

"We are on Stychs."

✦

Your Royal Highness, Sir:

Per your command, sire, I have ventured to the Westfront Range. I am loathe to report that while the land itself is interesting and even fruitful, there is about it something uncanny and unsettling. An alien magic permeates the atmosphere. Never has any king taken this land, nor do I see that you would gain sufficient benefit therefrom to justify the cost in blood and treasure to conquer it.

I will report more fully upon my return. Until then, may all health and happiness be yours, my true King.

~Sir Condran, Knight Royal of the Realm

THREE

"What?" Grey and I exclaimed in unison, and he exploded to his feet. In no time, he was standing next to me.

But Xyla fell back into her stupor.

My blood pounded in my ears, and I had to take calming breaths to try to gather my thoughts.

"I need to make a bow," Grey said, irrelevantly. "Whatever is wrong with her isn't going to get better if she's not eating."

I just nodded numbly. What did I care about some stupid bow? We were on Stychs, wherever...whatever that was. I wanted to shake the dragon awake and make her explain it to me.

But the sense of Grey's comment eventually penetrated my thoughts. He was right. We all needed to eat. I could at least get water heating, ready for Traz's return.

I filled my saucepan with the last of the water from my waterskin. While it heated, I went to a nearby stream where melted snow from the mountaintops made its bubbling, sparkling way to the valley far below.

And the stream was right where it should be. That made me feel a little more grounded. Xyla must be wrong. We couldn't be anywhere but back home. Two different places simply couldn't be identical. Could they?

I shook these thoughts out of my mind. Several splashes of the cold water onto my face made me feel more awake and clearheaded. Whatever happened had just muddled all of our thinking, even Xyla's. Poor thing. If she'd been hit by lightning, no wonder she was disoriented.

When I got back to the cave, Traz stood there holding four rabbits, but with a worried expression on his face. When he saw me, it dissolved into relief.

"Where'd you go?" he demanded. "I got back and no one was here…" His voice trailed off. So, I thought, he was unsettled, too.

"Just filling my waterskin." I held it up. "Hey, good catch!"

He shrugged. "Where's Grey?"

"Went to find some wood to make a new bow. You're not going to be able to keep a dragon fed, even if you are the deadliest shot in the world."

"I could bring down an elk as good as Grey can," he said with an indignant look.

"Yes, yes," I said quickly, "I'm sure you can. And Grey will be able to use your help."

"Use his help with what?" Grey came striding in carrying a long, curved branch.

"With the hunting. Traz has already caught us a good meal."

Traz raised the rabbits so Grey could see, then went outside to skin them. I hoped he'd hurry so we could get them roasting quickly.

"I don't need his help," Grey said, a bit bad-temperedly as he sat down near the fire and started fiddling with the branch, turning it this way and that and testing its flex. "I can't believe I just dropped my best bow like that. This one won't even come close."

After awhile Traz came back in with the rabbits ready to cook. He'd made a spit, which he tended with great care. He'd been a kitchen boy at Roylinn Academy, where my brother Breyard and I had studied magic before we'd been caught up with Xyla and the mages, and he was a much better cook than I was. Soon, the delicious odor of roasting meat filled the air, making me feel light-headed with hunger.

Without warning, Grey snapped, "When is that meat going to be ready?" By now, he'd started working on the branch with one of his knives, and a pile of wood shavings lay in front of him.

"Be patient," Traz said, just as testily. "It takes awhile to cook it to a proper succulence."

"I don't care about succulence!" The vehemence in Grey's tone surprised me. I'd never seen him lose patience with anyone or anything before.

"Fine," said Traz, reaching for one of the sticks holding a rabbit. He removed it from the spit, being careful not to let the others drop into the fire. He held the stick out to Grey, who took it a little hesitantly. "Don't complain to me if it's undercooked. You want yours now, too, Donavah?"

I glanced from one to the other, the tension thick between them. "Uh, no, that's all right. I'll wait."

Grey set the partly whittled branch on the ground and went outside. I took a step to follow him, but then Traz made an impatient sound and said, "Jerk. He always ruins everything."

"He does not! He's just hungry."

"And we're not?"

"Who's being surly now? Look, Traz, we're all hungry and tired and confused. Can't you hurry those rabbits up a bit? We'll feel better once we've eaten."

With a sigh, he turned back to the fire.

+ + +

After Traz and I had finished eating, I went outside to talk to Grey but couldn't find him. Wondering where he'd gone—and why—I went back inside where it was warmer. I took my meditation kit out of my pack and went deeper into the cave. It was too dark to tell what colors the candles were until I lit them, when I found that I'd somehow picked two that were the same: ivory for peace. Using a matched pair, although the tradition among magicians, wasn't the most powerful use of magic, so I blew one out and selected another: lavender for clarity.

It was hard to clear my mind, harder than ever before. I could feel the rhythm of life, but couldn't seem to align myself to it. I concentrated harder, thinking that if I could only catch the beat, I would be able to proceed with the meditation routine.

Cacophony pressed in on me. For a moment, I thought I would go mad from the disruption of my spirit. The sound tugged me in opposite directions, threatening to rip my sanity to pieces.

Lights of red, green, and blue spiraled around me, driving me to distraction without providing illumination.

Then the gentlest of touches on my psyche. I focused on

it, willing myself not to lose contact. I didn't question what it was. It had a sweet taste and sensuous odor that drew me toward it.

Bit by bit, my spirit moved through the ether, nudging itself into rhythm with this world. With each passing moment, I felt more and more at one, once again, with nature around me.

Then, with a psychic jolt, my soul fell into the proper rhythm, and the world blossomed around me. Overcome with the richness of it all, my senses momentarily closed up and everything went black.

And quiet. And still.

I floated on the nothingness.

Then a whisper of wind formed into melodious words.

"Ah. What have we here? Who are you?"

I said nothing.

"Such power. Power that is raw and young and beautiful. Such power as I crave. Where are you?"

And still I said nothing.

"You refuse to answer? I have tasted you. I shall find you."

Tentacles of thought exploded the blackness. My spirit recoiled, and my body crashed to the floor.

I sat up, feeling a bit dizzy. When I scrunched my eyes closed, the whole world felt like it was spinning, but it wasn't much better with them open.

I put out the candles and sat for a few minutes, waiting for everything to return to normal.

Then Grey was there. He placed a supportive hand on my back and said, "Are you all right?"

A different sort of confusion flooded through me. All of my attention focused on his touch.

"Donavah? Are you all right?" he repeated.

"Um, yeah," I finally managed to say. "I think so."

"Come to the fire where it's warmer." He stood up and reached a hand down to me. I took it and let him pull me to my feet. "Your hands are as cold as ice! Let me make you something warm to drink."

I left the candles where they were and went with him, Grey still holding my hand in his.

Traz frowned at us from where he sat near the fire. He scowled without saying a word as Grey wrapped my cloak around my shoulders and helped me to sit down, then made me tea.

I was glad Grey didn't ask again about my meditation session, because for now, I didn't want to talk about it. Who did that voice belong to? It had been so soft and quiet I couldn't even tell if it was male or female. And what did it mean, "I shall find you"? The whole idea of meeting a stranger's spirit while meditating made me feel uneasy, as if someone had been poking around inside me.

Eventually, while Traz watched Grey working once again on his bow, I curled up next to the fire and went to sleep.

I woke up twice in the night. Once, the fire had burned down to embers, so I arose and stoked it up. The second time, just an hour or so before dawn, the fire was roaring and Grey was sitting up, working on his bow again. I pushed myself up onto one elbow. He glanced at me, then back at his work.

"The stars," he said, his voice so quiet that I barely heard him.

"What? What about the stars?"

"They're all in the right places."

I sat up and moved closer to him so we could talk without waking Traz up. "I'm not following you."

"Xyla said we were on another world, this Stychs place, but all the stars are exactly where they should be for this place at this time of year."

"Oh." The enormity of that hit me. "Then what do you think she meant?"

He looked over at her, a frown furrowing his brow. "I don't know. It's not like Malk taught me any dragon lore."

I yawned hugely.

"Sorry," he said with a half-smile. "I didn't mean to bore you."

"No, no," I said quickly. "Not bored. Just tired."

"Go back to sleep, then. We can talk more in the morning."

+ + +

When I awoke, Xyla still lay exactly where she'd stopped the night before, no change in her condition. Her tail did give a tiny flick when I placed a hand on her neck, though, and I took that as an encouraging sign. Traz was nowhere to be seen, and I guessed he was hunting again. Grey was outside, taking some practice shots with the now-completed bow.

"I wouldn't even use this to teach Traz to shoot," he said,

"but it'll have to do for now. I'll need to get a better one before long, if we can only find a settlement."

"Does that mean that you *will* teach him to shoot?" I asked hopefully.

"I suppose I will. If I can. If I must."

His eyes dared me to rise to the bait, but I didn't. "And you'll be able to bring down something big enough for Xyla to eat?"

Grey grimaced. "I hope so. I'll go now and see what I can find."

"Before breakfast? You have to eat something before you go."

"Already did. Leftover rabbit. Well, wish me good hunting."

And he disappeared into the woods.

I went back inside and made tea. Soon Traz returned with a pair of small birds, which we cooked up into a simple stew in my saucepan.

"We're going to miss bread before long," I observed.

"I already do."

"Grey mentioned trying to find a settlement so he could get a new bow. We could get bread, too."

"With what?" There was a hint of exasperation in his voice. "How much money do *you* have?"

I hadn't thought of that. "I see what you mean. I haven't any."

"Neither do I. If we even find a settlement, which I doubt, we'll have to work for anything we want to buy."

Xyla's weak voice interrupted. "Donavah?"

I ran over to her. "Xyla? Are you awake?"

"Hungry," she said.

"I know. Grey is out hunting right now." But when would

he be back? It was Winter, and finding anything worthwhile to bring back could take all day. Or longer.

"You must find the other dragons," she said, and somehow, her voice sounded a little stronger.

"What other dragons?"

"The other red dragons."

"But Xyla, there are no other red dragons. You're the only one."

"That was on Hedra. Now we're on Stychs."

There it was again. "What do you mean, Stychs? We're exactly where we were before, just everyone has gone." That sounded stupid even to me.

"No. We are on Stychs." There was a pause. "I cannot explain now. Perhaps later, when I am stronger."

I sighed. I wanted to understand her, and I wished that maejic extended to reading minds, not only being able to converse with animals.

When she'd fallen asleep again, I got my cloak and went outside. Opening my senses, I could now feel the life of the forest. Last night's meditation seemed to have done the trick.

I stepped into the woods and walked in among the trees. The slow life that pulsed through them felt much as it did at home, although there was a slightly different flavor that I couldn't quite define.

The smaller branches of the trees seemed to bend a little toward me, as if in greeting. I smiled as I raised my hands high above my head, touching the leaves I could reach. A ripple of gladness flowed out across the forest, and a tide of welcome returned.

Then a wave of hunger that had nothing to do with my own appetite washed over me. A mind-bending hunger that bordered on starvation. The scent of blood and flesh and bone. I put a hand to my head in a vain effort to dispel the feeling. Instead, it grew stronger.

I stumbled back to the cave, wondering what was wrong with me. Xyla stood half in, half out, and I caught her sense of anticipation. A moment later, with a dragging, almost crashing sound, Grey came out of the woods, pulling the carcass of a huge animal that I didn't recognize. I didn't mind Xyla eating, of course, but I didn't like to watch it, either, so I went into the cave. Grey followed, leaving Xyla to her meal, and I made some tea for him.

"That was fast," I said. "I didn't expect to see you back until this afternoon."

"I know. It was uncanny. There was no sign of any prey at all, much less something big enough for a dragon. Then, all of a sudden, there it was. Almost like magic."

"Or maybe maejic?" I laughed, then stopped abruptly at that thought.

He gave me a gentle smile. "Maybe."

"This is good. Is there more?" Xyla asked in a plaintive tone.

Grey rose to his feet. "No rest for the weary, I see. Hope I get that lucky again. This bow isn't up to any *real* hunting."

+ + +

By evening, Xyla was sleeping soundly, having eaten the first beast plus two more that Grey brought back. She still seemed weak, and she spoke very little, but there was at least some improvement.

Traz had returned near nightfall with enough meat for supper. I asked him what he'd been doing all day, but he just made a vague, meaningless noise and turned back to tending the meal as it cooked.

I watched him closely and saw that he kept stroking the stones we'd used to make a ring around the fire, as if trying to memorize their shapes or their texture. I almost asked him about it, but he sat with hunched shoulders, suggesting that he wished to be left alone.

Then, not long after we'd finished eating supper, we all heard footsteps approaching the cave.

✦

We turn our attention now to the most enduring of the creation myths, that of Etos.

It is said that his was the first power, the first life, the first being, and all power, life, and being sprang from him.

Before Etos, the world was black and void. He filled the world with his presence, and thereby filled it with color. Color covered the face of the earth, then reached into its soul and brought forth sound. Color and sound danced, and brought forth scent. Color, sound, and scent meditated and brought forth taste. These four laughed and brought forth touch.

And Etos was well-pleased.

And he sang of his pleasure.

And brought forth life.

And when he was finished, he settled deep into the ether to watch his creation live and dance and meditate and laugh and die and return to the earth from whence it sprang.

-from the lecture notes of Tandor

Four

✦

"H'lo? Who's there?"
Grey was on his feet, knife in hand, in a flash.
He stalked to the mouth of the cave, staying in the shadows.

A figure took a step inside. "H'lo?" the voice said again.
"I know you're there."

I could understand the words, but they were spoken with
a strange, unfamiliar accent.

Grey took advantage of the pause to pounce. He grabbed
the person from behind, one arm across their chest and the
other hand holding a knife to their throat.

I gasped in surprise; I'd never seen Grey like this—dangerous, lethal even, toward another person. The air tightened
with tension, but Xyla slept on, oblivious to it.

"Ya! Let go! I haven't done anything to you."

"Move," Grey growled. "Toward the fire. But don't try
anything."

They both came into the firelight, and I got a good look
at the person.

A very dark-skinned young woman just a few years older
than I stood there, her eyes sparkling with anger. She had long
hair that was brown or black, I couldn't tell for sure in the firelight, and was braided into many tiny braids. She was dressed
much as we were, in buckskin trousers and tunic though she

wore a jacket instead of a cloak. Like Grey, she had a knife hanging from her belt, giving her a dangerous air.

"I'm going to let you go now," he said, still speaking in a low, threatening voice, "but if you make a false move or try to get away, I'll kill you." And I believed he would.

"Why would I leave? I was trying to find you, in case you hadn't noticed."

Grey let her go, and she brushed off her clothes and rearranged them a bit. His eyes glittered as her hand strayed to her hip. She looked down and found the knife sheath empty, and when she looked back at Grey, he pulled a hand from behind his back and held up a wicked-looking knife.

With a shriek of outrage, she leapt at him, reaching for the weapon. Grey flicked it away, far out of her reach, but she didn't pay attention to that as she closed on him, fists flying.

His sardonic grin changed to a look of surprise at the ferocity of her attack. She landed one blow in his stomach and another on his chin before he quite realized what was happening.

Traz and I exchanged glances. He wore a delighted smile, just as one would expect from a boy watching a fight. I grabbed his shoulder.

"You're staying out of it," I hissed, not trusting him enough to let him go. He tried to shrug out of my grip, but I held on tighter. I knew Grey would win this fight, but I didn't want Traz to get hurt in the process.

By now, Grey had grasped the young woman's left wrist and was holding it over her head. But despite her awkward stance, she was still managing to keep her right arm free and get in a few more punches.

Her high-pitched screeches were punctuated by Grey's intermittent grunts as he tried to get her under control.

Their struggle moved them closer to the fire, and I cried out a warning to Grey. That broke his concentration, and she got him square on the jaw. I winced as if she'd actually struck me instead of him.

Now Grey got serious, using his greater height and weight to advantage. He swung her round by her left arm, pulling down abruptly to knock her off balance. Her scream of rage was cut off with an "oopf" as she tumbled to the ground. Grey scrambled to pin her down. She kicked at him, and Traz let out an indignant squawk when she almost got Grey where it counted.

But it was over a moment later. The woman lay beneath Grey, who used his weight to hold her down. They both were breathing heavily. She spit in Grey's face, and he shook it off.

"That's enough," he said in a loud, stern voice I scarcely recognized. "Donavah, get something to tie her hands."

She spit at him again.

I knew I didn't have any rope in my pack. "Traz, lend me your sling."

With a grin that suggested he was enjoying this far too much, he dug it out of his pocket and handed it to me.

The woman was still struggling against Grey, and I rushed over. He forced her wrists together, and I hesitantly started wrapping the thongs around them. Once satisfied she couldn't slip her hands out, Grey took over and bound her securely, then wiped off his face with a revolted expression. When she made a motion with her jaw as if she were going to spit yet again, Grey raised his hand as if to strike her.

"I'd rather not," he said. The venom in his voice sent a chill down my spine and even gave the woman pause. She swallowed.

Grey grabbed the collar of her shirt and pulled her to a sitting position. I stepped away because something about this woman unsettled me, and it didn't matter that her hands were bound.

She glanced over at me, and our eyes met. Her gaze pierced me, leaving me feeling as if she could read my soul.

"It was you," she said in a quiet voice.

I took another step back. "What was me?" I said the words so softly I wasn't even sure I spoke them aloud.

"I felt you. That's what drew me here."

Grey looked at me, a confused scowl on his face. Traz moved to my side, as if I needed his protection. I just shook my head.

Her lip curled and she shrugged in a disdainful way. "As you wish." She glared back at Grey. "What are you going to do with me now?"

He rose to his feet and started brushing the dirt off his clothes. "We'll have to wait and see. But I'm not going to hurt you, if that's what you mean."

"I'm *so* reassured."

Grey just threw her a dirty look and walked away.

Surprisingly, it was Traz who remembered his manners first. "I'm Traz," he said. "What's your name?"

"Why would I be wanting to tell you that?"

Annoyance began to take the edge off my fear. "Is politeness something you don't do around here?"

She let out a snort of disgust and raised her bound hands toward me in answer. Perhaps she had a point there. Still, if she hadn't attacked Grey, she wouldn't be in this predicament now.

Undeterred, Traz went over to the fire and looked in the supper pot sitting next to it. "Well, luckily Donavah hasn't gotten around to washing the dishes yet. There's not much, but you can have what's left." He scraped out the last bits of stew gravy into a bowl and handed it to her.

Her eyes softened a little as she took the food and awkwardly slurped it out of the bowl. I moved closer to the fire, hoping its warmth would chase away some of the chill that this woman brought to my heart.

+ + +

Grey took the first watch. When he woke me, he merely commented that our captive had neither slept nor spoken. Then he wrapped himself in his cloak and lay down.

I sat across the fire from the woman. She stared at me, and I shivered. Was she trying to read my mind or something? All my senses were alert, but nothing disturbed the life vibrations except her anger, and that was understandable enough.

After awhile, she spoke, not making any effort to keep her voice down. "Your boyfriend is a prick, but the kid's not bad."

"My boyfriend?" I asked with a surprised gulp. My face burned. "He's not—"

"Uh huh," she interrupted. "If he's not, you wish he was, don't you?"

My eyes shot to where Grey lay. I hoped he'd fallen asleep and would stay that way. My feelings for him weren't something I wanted discussed, not with the stranger or anyone else, much less in front of him.

"So what's wrong with the dragon?" she asked.

"Huh?" Could this possibly be a more disconcerting conversation? "How do you know there's something wrong with her?"

The woman rolled her eyes.

"It's pretty obvious to anyone with the wit to perceive it." Her tone implied that I lacked that wit.

Xyla stirred just then, as if our talking about her penetrated her sleep. Her eyes, half open, glittered in the firelight. I wanted to go over to her, to touch her, to try to lend her strength, but I needed to keep an eye on this woman.

She looked over at the dragon, too, and when she did, the hard look melted from her face. Then she let out a startled gasp. "Xyla says I must lead you to Delaron."

My insides froze. Xyla had spoken to this woman. And hadn't included me.

Then to me Xyla said, "She is not a danger. She will help you."

I rose to my feet, torn between not wanting to take my eyes off the woman and wanting the comfort of being close to the dragon.

"But Xyla," I said, "she attacked Grey. She would've killed him if she could've."

"She understands now. You can trust her. She will help." And the pinpoints of reflected firelight disappeared as Xyla closed her eyes.

When the woman turned back to me, her face was no longer angry. "My name is Shandry," she said. "I will do as Xyla says."

I plopped back down. How could Xyla be so sure this Shandry could be trusted? Could I bring myself to trust her? She'd practically admitted that it was her spirit I'd met while meditating, that she'd sought us out because of that.

Xyla's voice inside my head cut through my confusion. "Untie her," she commanded in a tone that was not to be contradicted.

I swallowed, trying to suppress my own feelings. Then I went over to Shandry, who watched my every move with a completely unreadable look on her face.

"Xyla says I'm to untie you." I wanted it to be very clear that this was the dragon's idea, not mine. I crouched next to Shandry, and she held out her hands to me.

As I fiddled with the knot, I saw that for all his anger, Grey hadn't been cruel in binding her wrists. It was cleverly done, the way he'd made it so she couldn't possibly free herself, but in a way that wasn't painful and didn't cut off the circulation. It took a frustratingly long time to loosen the knots. More than once I was tempted to cut them, but I had a feeling that ruining Traz's sling would be a mistake. Not only would it mean one less hunting implement—which we couldn't afford to lose in our current circumstances—but also he would kill me.

My heart beat hard in my chest and my hands shook as I unwound the leather thongs from Shandry's wrists. What if

Xyla were wrong? What if Shandry ran off? What if she tried to kill me? I didn't have the first idea of how to defend myself.

Shandry leapt to her feet as soon as I'd freed her. I did, too, letting out a yelp of surprise. She headed for the mouth of the cave, and I raced after her, scarcely noticing the sounds of Grey and Traz behind me.

"Where are you going?" I shouted at her.

She paused just inside and glanced back at me with a scowl. "To relieve myself, of course." And she carried on outside.

I came to a stop as Grey dashed up to my side.

"What's going on?" he demanded.

I gulped. Now I'd have to admit what I'd done. "Xyla told me to untie her," I said in a quiet voice, not wanting to say the words at all.

"What?" Grey's shout echoed around the cave. He took my upper arms in a painful grip. "Are you mad? How could you let that viper go free?"

I cringed before his wrath. I hated it when anyone was angry at me, and this was worse than ever. I didn't even try to get away from him.

"I just did what Xyla told me to do," I said as tears rose to my eyes.

He gave me a disgusted look that made me want to crawl into a hole in the ground. But before he could start shouting again, Traz walked up holding Shandry's knife. "At least she doesn't have this," he said.

Grey let go of me, almost as if he were throwing me away, and took the knife from Traz.

"I'll be having that back," Shandry said, walking back in at that moment.

"No, you won't," Grey growled, glaring at her and holding the knife in such a way that she couldn't try to take it from him.

Xyla let out a snort that froze us all. "Enough!" her voice bellowed in my head. In Grey's and Shandry's, too, to judge by the startled expressions on their faces. "Shandry will lead you to Delaron, where you will find aid for me. Grey will stay behind to hunt for me. You will trust one another as I trust you. And you will stop disturbing me with this pointless agitation."

She hadn't said anything aloud, but, as if the outburst used up the last of her reserves, a stunned silence fell in the cave.

Traz broke it. "What? What did she say?"

Grey's only answer was to grab Shandry's upper arm and guide her back inside to the fire. Traz and I followed, me wiping the tears from my cheeks and hoping Traz didn't notice.

I hated it that Grey had shouted at me that way. It just reinforced the difference in our ages, that he thought he could treat me like a child. And it made me actually feel like a child, too. In my misery, I almost missed the half-smile Shandry gave Grey as she glanced at his hand on her arm and then at his face.

We all sat around the fire, Grey fiddling casually with Shandry's knife.

She was the first to speak, and honey practically dripped from her tone. "Shall we start over again? I'm Shandry. You all are?"

Grey pointed the tip of the knife at each of us as he spoke our names.

"And you're here because?" Shandry asked as if she were a hostess at a tea party.

"I'll ask the questions, if you don't mind," Grey snapped.

Shandry gave him a sweet smile and lifted her hand in agreement.

Grey's face relaxed ever so slightly, but the rest of his body was as alert as a hunting cat's. I just sat quietly, listening to the conversation but not taking part, not wanting to draw Grey's attention back to me.

"Who exactly are you?" Grey asked.

I expected Shandry to give him a sarcastic answer, but Xyla's commands seemed to have put her into a different frame of mind. "I'm not anyone, really," she said, "just a simple peasant living alone in my cottage nearby."

Grey raised the knife. "Not so simple, I imagine. But carry on."

"There isn't much to say. I do live quite alone, whether you wish to believe me or not."

"Then why did you come here? I can hardly believe you'd just gone out for an evening walk in the woods."

"No, I was seeking out the source of the disruption in the forest's life force."

I looked at her closely. It must have been her. Who else could it be? Why had she sought me out? The voice had said something about craving my power. I huddled deeper into my cloak and thoughts, closing myself off to her.

As if reading my mind, Grey asked, "But that still doesn't explain why you're here."

Shandry's eyes blazed as if she were beginning to lose patience. "Look, the dragon is satisfied with my being here. Surely you don't think I fancy doing what she asked, leading a bunch of strangers on a journey across the mountains at this time of year, do you? And since I'm the one being inconvenienced, I think I have a right to know some things about who you are and why you're here, too."

Before Grey could reply, Traz said, "She's right, you know. It's only fair."

I shook my head, though no one noticed. I didn't want her to know anything about us. Grey summed up our story, telling Shandry more than I would've liked but less than he could have.

When he was done, Shandry, speaking in a soft and quiet voice, said, "You're not from here. I didn't understand when Xyla first told me, but I see it now. You're not from here at all. You're from there."

✦

Dragons were not always here. For many long ages, there were none such as these.

Serpents, yes. And lizards, and other creepy-crawly things. Birds aloft on wing. And all other beasts needful to populate the world.

And then came the dragons.

One moment, they were not. Next moment, they were.

None knew whence they came.

None knew how.

None knew why.

None knew the place they would take in our world. Or if they would ever leave us and return to their home.

~from the teachings of Gedden, lore master

FIVE

Unable to stand it any longer, I shouted, "Here? There? Where?" The sound echoed around the cave, startling Traz and Grey.

Shandry shot me an indecipherable look, one that made my skin crawl. Then her eyes took on a dreamy cast, and after a long pause, she began to speak in a sing-song sort of voice.

"Many, many long years ago, an age ago, the red dragons came to us. Civil war had broken out in their home, and to escape destruction, they came here, to Stychs." My heart skipped a beat, then started up in double-time. "At first, they were seen as interlopers, a threat to the perfect balance that had long been sought and only recently found. Although they could breathe fire, they chose not to use it against the peoples and creatures of this world. They went to Delaron to dwell there in the desert with the sages until such time as they could return to their own world. And they did not disrupt the perfect balance. In the end, they contributed their own knowledge and wisdom, so that eventually, the sages realized that they were an integral part of the balance. Now they are revered. And so it has been from then until now." At this point, she shook her head a little, and her voice lost that recitation quality. "But it has always been said that one day, the dragons would return to their own world. When they were summoned back by one of their own." She turned and looked at Xyla.

I stared first at Shandry, then at Xyla. "How," I started, and it came out as a squeak. I tried again. "How could Xyla…bring us to another world?"

"That I cannot say. You will have to ask the sages."

"The who?"

Shandry sighed. "The sages. At Delaron. Where Xyla has told me to take you. The red dragons live there."

Grey cut in. "All right. It's clear that Xyla wants the three of you to go. How long is this journey?"

"I'd guess about two weeks this time of year. Maybe longer if the weather doesn't cooperate. It's not like there will be caravans going over the pass this early in the season, so we won't be able to hitch a ride."

"Two weeks?" I exclaimed. "Isn't there a faster way?"

Shandry shrugged. "As far as I can tell, we can't exactly fly."

My heart sank. Despite her sarcasm, she was right. Which meant another journey. On foot. With someone I didn't trust. I looked over at Xyla who hadn't moved.

Grey rubbed his eyes. "Let's pick this up again tomorrow. Donavah, why don't you finish your watch." He might as well have said something about botching my first one; the message was loud and clear in the tone of his voice. "Then the usual rotation."

Before long, everyone but me was sound asleep. I stared at the fire, trying to make sense of everything that had happened in this long, confusing day.

The peacefulness of sleep settled through the cave, and I had a hard time keeping my eyes open. The flames danced before me, snapping and popping in a syncopated rhythm.

They seemed to drain my worries and anxieties, leaving me feeling calm and open. I struggled to stay awake.

The outline of a face appeared in the fire. It started as a vaguely head-shaped outline, but soon the features grew clear. My heart skipped when I recognized Anazian, the traitor mage.

His words filled my mind. "The game board is set. It's your move."

As always in the dream, I didn't reply.

Then his rollicking poured through me. "Perhaps you should give up and go home. Yes, that would be a plan. Home, where all is not as you left it." The laughter turned brittle. "Go to your mama and papa, where you are truly needed. If it's not too late." His evil chortle filled my mind, my ears, the cave, the whole world. And then it faded away. The last thing I heard was, "Your move."

Home. I must go home to Mama and Papa. I rose to my feet and went outside. There was no discernable path, so I pushed my way through the trees. Branches caught at my clothes and snagged them. Twigs scratched my face. But I kept on.

Which way was Barrowfield? I looked up to try to see the stars, but the trees were too thick overhead. I couldn't even see the moon. Or perhaps it hadn't risen yet, or had already set.

Panic set in. What had Anazian done to my family? And why? I moved faster, the need to get home pressing on me like an unbearable weight.

Fear darkened my vision, and it became harder and harder to move forward. Once, I struck my head on an overhanging branch. I stubbed my toes on rocks, biting back yelps of pain so that Anazian wouldn't be able to find me.

The trees themselves seemed to be working against me, impeding my progress. I tried to summon my maejic so I could command them to assist me, but it was gone. Anazian had taken my maejic. Again.

Tears streamed down my face, making it even harder to see. But I couldn't stop my feet from running.

Both my heart and my body grew cold, and I no longer felt the pain of crashing into things. Faster and faster I moved, until a large object tripped me up and I fell in a heap, striking my head on something hard.

+ + +

Someone was shaking me. "Donavah. Wake up. C'mon, wake up."

I opened my eyes to find myself lying in mud next to a fallen log. I was so cold I could hardly move.

The someone shook me again. I struggled to sit up, and strong arms helped, then began wrapping me in a cloak—my cloak.

"Are you all right?" And now I recognized Shandry's voice.

I peered at her, to find her looking at me with a concerned expression.

"Are you all right?" she repeated.

My teeth chattered so I could hardly speak. "I ... I think so. What hap ... hap ... happened?"

"Let's get you moving first. Can you stand?"

Barely. I certainly couldn't have without her help. We started walking slowly, carefully, back to the cave. I leaned against Shandry, and she kept an arm around my shoulders, guiding me along the way and using her free hand to push branches aside.

"I couldn't sleep and decided to try to find some water to drink, and I found you dozing next to the fire."

I groaned. I'd fallen asleep on watch. Even in my confused and half-frozen state, my heart sank.

"When you got up and went out without putting on anything warm, I thought you must be walking in your sleep. And you were moving fast. I grabbed your cloak and followed, but I lost you when you started running. Lucky for you it didn't take me long to find you once you fell."

"Grey will kill me when he finds out I fell asleep on watch."

"Then we won't tell him."

My ability to think seemed to be thawing. "Why are you helping me?"

"I couldn't just let you die. You would've, you know, on a night like this with nothing to keep you warm."

"A few hours ago, I bet you wouldn't have minded letting me die."

After a short pause, Shandry said, "Not strictly true. I might not mind letting Grey die. But I don't have anything against you. Watch your step there." She steered me around a small boulder.

"Grey's not so bad," I replied.

"Hmm. Maybe not," she said in a suggestive tone that I didn't like one bit.

Back in the cave, I sat near the fire while Shandry heated some water. I drank it without bothering to make it into tea. Then I got a rag from my pack and used the rest of the warm water to clean the mud from my face and hands, and as much from my clothes as I could. It wouldn't do for Grey to notice it and ask. When I felt recovered enough, I woke Traz up and lay down to sleep until my next watch.

+ + +

In the morning, both Shandry and Grey moved slowly and stiffly, as if they were in pain, though neither of them would admit it. Shandry was true to her word, not saying anything to Grey or Traz about my lapse the night before. We were all hungry, which didn't improve our irritated tempers. Still, we had to start planning this journey Xyla had set us to.

Grey, bruises purpling on his face from the previous night's fight, took charge. "There are two main things," he said. "The route to get to Delaron, and supplies for the road."

"As far as the route," Shandry said, "I know the way. There's a road not far from here that goes over the mountain pass and down to the desert. Delaron is a little less than two weeks journey by foot into the desert."

Grey gave a curt nod. "Which leads directly to the question of supplies. We," his finger sketched a little circle in the air indicating himself, Traz, and me, "don't have anything."

"Again, not a problem," Shandry said, giving Grey a flirtatious smile that set my teeth on edge. "I have supplies at my cottage. And a pony we can use to carry the baggage. Speaking of which, I need to get back soon to feed him."

"So it's just as simple as that?" Grey asked, his tone heavy with suspicion. "Last night you try to kill me, and this morning you're willing to leave everything behind to help us?"

Shandry's shoulders drooped a little, and she looked down at her hands. "Well, you know, it's a chance to get away, do something different."

I opened my mouth to ask what she meant, but Grey made a motion with his hand and I remained silent. In a low, neutral voice, he asked the question himself.

When she raised her head, the expression on her face was bleak. "Do you know what it's like to be alone—truly alone? To never have anyone to talk to, to do things with? Because that's what my life is. Looking after myself, a pony, and a bit of garden. Seeing other people twice a year when I stock up on supplies, and them not wanting to talk to me beyond setting the price of goods. Have you ever been just plain tired of your own company?"

I felt the anger go out of Grey at these words. "Yes," he said softly, and I knew it to be true. "Actually, I do know."

"Then you should understand. I'm sorry about last night and all, but we *did* catch each other by surprise. Can't you get past it?"

Grey took a deep breath and let it out again. "Xyla said to trust you." The struggle he was having with himself was obvious. I bit my lower lip, waiting for him to reply.

"All right," he said.

Shandry nodded solemnly.

After that, things began to happen quickly. Grey decided that he and Shandry would go to her cottage to get the pony and supplies. She practically glowed at that suggestion, telling Grey he could have one of her bows and a proper quiver full of arrows, and a bad feeling grew in my stomach. Or, more accurately, in my heart. Traz would hunt for our evening meal, and I would keep watch. Stupid job, I thought, as I watched Grey and Shandry walk off together. What exactly was I supposed to do if someone came? Fend them off with my nonexistent fighting skills? I couldn't even defend myself, much less an unconscious dragon, and thinking back to Shandry and Grey's fight the night before didn't help me feel any better.

I had such mixed feelings about Shandry. She was strong and capable, much like Grey. And while she seemed to have a heart as hard as rock, she'd been kind to me when there wasn't any reason to be. She was also pretty and closer to Grey's age than I was. He had a lot more in common with her than he did with me. After half a day in her company, he'd probably never spare me another thought.

Well, at least Xyla's plan meant that Grey would be staying behind while Shandry took Traz and me on the journey to this Delaron place.

Sitting alone while the others were gone, letting my imagination run away with itself—especially on the subject of Grey and Shandry—didn't improve my mood. And my fear was realized when I heard their laughter as they came back.

Shandry led a tan-colored pony who was laden with a large number of packs and bundles. The pony seemed loathe to come inside, and I couldn't figure out why until it struck me that he must be afraid of Xyla.

"C'mon, Dyster," Shandry said, tugging on his reins. "It's all right. She won't eat you."

I wasn't so sure about that, but the poor beast couldn't spend the night outside. "Maybe we should put him in one of the other caves," I suggested.

"Good idea," Grey said.

Once we'd unloaded everything and took it all inside, I led the way to the nearest cave, where Shandry unbridled Dyster, hobbled him, and filled his nosebag. Then we went back to the main cave without either of us having said a word.

Grey was in the midst of sorting which things were staying and which were going. He showed me a bow, exhibiting far more enthusiasm than necessary.

"This is much better than that one I made. It's probably better than the one I left behind. And it's only Shandry's *third*-best bow."

"Oh?" I asked in a dry tone. "She didn't give you her best?"

"No," he said, "she'll need her best ones for your trip."

He really didn't get it. I turned away from him to the stores they'd brought. Potatoes, flour, apples, nuts. More cooking gear. A few loaves of bread. Sweetening and jars of preserved fruit. Grey would eat like a king. Shandry took a few things and busied herself at the fire, making something to go with the roasted rabbits.

Dinner turned out to be delicious. There was a pot of hot grain that looked like porridge but had a strong barley flavor. Instead of butter for the bread, there was something that Shandry called *leten*, a beige-colored paste with a slight cinnamon flavor. There was also a hot drink that had an orangeish tinge and a spicy flavor, with much more zip than the morning tea I was used to. Traz and Grey both had second and third helpings.

Xyla slept on. Everything about her seemed out of kilter. Her heartbeat was strong and steady now, and she wasn't in any pain, but she simply couldn't seem to get into any sort of rhythm of life. It was as if she were juddering along, a half-beat behind everyone else.

Shandry seemed genuinely concerned, and that made me feel a little better disposed to her. Whether I liked it or not, we were going to be traveling together for a few weeks, and we were going to have to get along.

+ + +

Next morning, before we left, Grey took Traz aside and said something to him, to which Traz responded with a solemn nod. It was easy to guess that Grey was telling Traz to look after Shandry and me. It annoyed me that Grey thought I needed looking after by a young boy, until I realized that he'd done it merely as a kind gesture toward Traz.

Then the three of us who were going made ready to go.

Xyla lifted her head and said, "You will have success, Donavah."

"I hope so. I don't know what we'll do if this doesn't work."

"Do not worry. It will work."

Her certainty made me suspicious. "Do you know something you're not telling me?"

"Go now, little one. I am hungry."

On the last comment, Grey's head jerked up. "Off with you, now," he said. "I need to get going myself. Don't want a hungry dragon on my hands." He grinned.

Then we were all saying goodbye. I hoped Grey would kiss my cheek, but he didn't. He stood in front of the cave and waved when I looked back one last time. Shandry led on, and Traz and I followed.

✦

*A half-played game of Talisman and Queen lies before
me, the jewel pieces glowing as they sit on the black velvet,
embroidered with glittering silver thread. The Queen's Heart,
made of diamond, gleams at the center. Ranged about are
the Talismans: mine, garnet; my opponent's, opal.*

*I cannot see against whom I play. Shrouded in shadow,
the brooding presence lies as if in sleep, absorbing energy
and my concentration. It seems to suck the very air from
the room. I can scarce breathe.*

*The game is almost won. My heart tells me that with
a single move, I will Secure the Queen's Heart. But my
brain is frozen, unable to make sense of the game pieces. A
wrong move, and my enemy will take all.*

*A voice breaks the silence—a familiar male voice that
echoes around the room growing in power instead of fading
away.*

"Your move," it says.

*Lightning begins to flash. The sky gleams blood red in
between flashes.*

*"The game board is set. It is your move," the voice says
again, taking the last of the air with it.*

I fall into a black pit of nothingness.

And then I awake.

Six

The first day passed unremarkably. I wasn't sure if I thought that was an omen of good things ahead or otherwise. The road was easy enough to follow as it carved a wide path clear of the surrounding woods. It was a new experience for me, traveling by foot but not having to carry a heavy pack. I could get used to this, I thought, watching Dyster being led by Shandry. I'd tried to speak to the pony, but he turned out not to be very talkative.

All morning, Traz marched well ahead of us, twirling his staff endlessly—before him, above his head, to one side, then the other. It made me dizzy watching. I wanted to tell him to stop, but what harm could there be in it? Besides, it would just ruin his fun to no good purpose.

Around midday, we stopped for lunch. As I'd noticed before when traveling by foot, the simple food tasted better than expected, as if the exertion of the outdoor exercise improved the flavor. Or maybe just the appetite. But the day was cold, and we didn't stop for long.

Shandry cast an eye at the sky above the mountaintops ahead of us. "I don't like the look of those clouds rolling in," she said.

I looked where she pointed to see a dark bank of clouds.

"Maybe we should've waited, not left so soon." I didn't like the idea of traveling in a storm.

She shook her head. "No point in that, really. It's early Spring and there will be storms. Can't do anything about it except wait a few months. And I'm thinking waiting wasn't really an option, was it?"

"No," I said, shaking my head at the thought of not doing anything at all for Xyla. "Not an option." I gritted my teeth. We'd just have to deal with whatever the weather threw at us.

The breeze began to pick up. A gust caught Traz's staff mid-twirl and blew it out of his grasp. He let out an almost pained cry when it struck the ground, as if he could feel the impact himself. I was going to have to talk to him about this strange obsession he'd developed.

We caught up with him as he brushed the staff off. "Maybe it's time to give it a rest," I said. "You've been thrashing that thing around all day. If you keep it up much longer, your arms might fall off."

He started to object, then caught my eye and grinned. "You're probably right, Mother."

Well before dark, Shandry insisted on finding a place to camp for the night. "This time of year," she said, "and this high up, storms can blow in fast. We want to be sure we're in a good place before dark."

"You think it's going to rain tonight?" Traz asked.

"I'll be surprised if it doesn't. Feels like it might even snow. We'll want to find someplace sheltered."

So even though it was still at least an hour before nightfall, we started looking for a likely spot. The road went through a small clearing that had a huge boulder along one side. If we positioned ourselves in the lee of the boulder, we would escape the worst of the wind.

"No," Traz said, his voice full of certainty. "There's something better a little farther along."

Shandry gave him a sharp look. "How do you know that?" I wondered exactly the same thing myself.

"I dunno," Traz said with a shrug. "I just do. It's that way." He pointed the staff away from the road, a little to the north.

Shandry sniffed. "Well, I don't know this part of the mountains well, but I'm sure I know them better than you do. And I say we stay here and make camp now."

Both of them looked at me, obviously expecting me to cast the deciding vote. What should I do? Shandry was right that Traz couldn't possibly know the terrain around here, but experience had taught me to trust him. I frowned.

"I don't know, Traz. This seems like a good spot. If it turns out you're wrong, we might not have time to get back here."

He gave me a look as if I'd just slapped him across the face. "But … but … " he spluttered. "Oh, fine. Side with her." He whirled around and stomped off in the direction he'd pointed.

Shandry rolled her eyes. "What's up with him? He's generally the sensible one."

I ignored the jibe. "He's usually right about these things."

"So go off with him," she said, turning away from me and securing Dyster's reins to a nearby tree.

Now what to do? Stay and help Shandry set up camp, or go find Traz? Had he actually gone to find this shelter he believed was there, or had he just gone off to sulk? I took a deep breath and let it out again.

"I'm going to get Traz," I said.

"Suit yourself." Shandry began kicking leaves and stones aside.

I went off in the direction Traz had gone. I couldn't track him, as that wasn't a skill I'd even begun to learn. But I had learned how to distinguish individual life vibrations back on Hedra, and I'd practiced most on Traz, so surely I could find him that way now. I unblocked.

The vibrations of the forest here were much like back home on Hedra, but there was a subtle difference, like the scent of an unfamiliar spice. The trees spoke to my heart, luring me on to explore their secrets.

I forced myself to concentrate. I had to find Traz. Where was his vibration in all this residue?

Then, like an almost-forgotten scent, there it was. Just the tiniest thread, and I followed it. Stepping carefully, trying not to make any noise, I moved forward. But it was impossible to walk quietly. Old dead leaves and dried twigs crunched underfoot. Still, I made a game of trying.

I imagined my maejic sinking down into my feet, dampening any noise my steps might make, eliminating all sign of my passing. It didn't work at first, not while I kept my mind on it. But once I gave up trying, my footsteps grew quiet. It was as if the trying were the thing that interfered with letting the maejic work.

I finally caught up with Traz near a small cliff face. He was leaning against an old stump, hunched over something in his hands. He started when I cleared my throat to announce my presence and he hastily shoved the thing into his pack.

"There," he said, pointing to an opening in the cliff. "I told you."

I scowled, first at the cave and then at Traz. "I don't understand. How did you know?"

He shook his head. "I dunno. I can't explain. I just knew there was a better spot than Shandry found, and that it was here."

"Well, it *is* better," I agreed.

"So we can go back and tell her?"

"Careful, Traz. She might not like being proved wrong."

"But Donavah, it's going to rain any minute now. Or snow. Wouldn't you rather be warm and dry in a cave than stuck next to a big rock with nothing more than some trees covering us?"

"When you put it that way—"

"Then c'mon. I'll race you back."

He made as if to dash off, but I put a hand on his arm to stop him. "Wait, Traz. Walk with me. Look, we're just getting started on this journey, and we need Shandry. I don't want to alienate her our first night out."

"Well, I don't want to freeze our first night out." A frown creased his forehead.

"I know it seems hard. But isn't one uncomfortable night worth it to keep the peace?"

"No! Not when I'm right and you know it! Why are you siding with her, anyway?"

That was a good question. I certainly didn't fancy spending a wet night out in the open when I didn't have to. On the other hand, I couldn't exactly explain to Traz that the last thing in the world I wanted was for Shandry to leave us stranded and go back to Grey.

We walked on for about ten minutes. Without warning, Traz threw out an arm to stop me and froze in place. My senses came fully alert, and I unblocked to try to sense the danger. Traz made a motion with his hand that I somehow knew meant not to move or make a sound. If my heart thudding in my chest didn't count.

He moved his head around this way and that, though it didn't seem he was actually looking at anything. He took a careful, soundless step, then another. I bit my lower lip in the effort not to follow. His head swiveled round at me and he mouthed, "Supper." Relief flooded me.

Not wanting to scare our meal away, I didn't follow him. Traz moved slowly, stealthy as a cat, each foot placed with care so as not to make a sound. The motion of his body was fluid, as if he moved to a music I couldn't hear.

Before long, he disappeared into the trees. I hadn't been standing there long, but I began to feel the cold. Chill and damp quickly seeped into my muscles, stiffening my joints. But whatever it was Traz had sensed—and how had he?—I didn't want to frighten it away.

The next few moments stretched out as if they were hours while I debated whether to shout for him. Or for Shandry.

Then there was a loud rustling amongst the trees, and a shout of triumph. Traz reappeared, holding up some small, dead beast, his impudent grin almost glowing in the failing light.

"Supper," he proclaimed, brandishing the carcass aloft as he walked up to me.

"What is it?" I asked.

"Dunno."

We examined it as we walked. It was about the size of a housecat though much broader. It had wicked-looking claws, black eyes, and long, sharp fangs. The thick pelt was dark brown, though where the light caught it, it gleamed gold.

"Strange-looking thing," I said. "I wonder if it's good eating."

"We'll find out soon enough, won't we?"

"Yeah. Good job hunting. How did you know it was there?"

Traz frowned and didn't say anything for several steps. "I don't know. I just did."

"That seems to be your answer to an awful lot of questions today."

He gave me a look of confusion mixed with a little fear. "Something weird is happening. Ever since we got here."

Traz, afraid of something? I couldn't remember him ever being afraid. Not of flying on Xyla the very first time, not of the Royal Guardsman who'd struck his face with a horsewhip, not even when we'd been attacked by the dragonmasters. What could possibly frighten him now?

"What?" I asked. "What's been happening?"

His shoulders hunched a little. "Just weird stuff. Things feel different than ever before."

"Like what? Do you feel sick or something?"

"No, I mean feel like in touching. When I touch things with my hands, they feel—I don't know—more alive than back home. Even things that aren't living. Like … " His voice trailed off.

"Like the staff?" I finished for him.

He nodded. "I know, it sounds stupid."

"No, it doesn't. I don't understand it, but it doesn't sound stupid." I put an arm around his shoulders companionably. "Whatever it is, just … let it flow."

He looked up at me with an expression of hope and relief. "You think so?"

"Didn't you say before you wanted to be maejic?" His eyes widened as he nodded. "Well, what you describe doesn't sound like that, but who knows what it might be? C'mon, it's starting to get dark. Let's hurry."

We didn't speak the rest of the way. Traz had given me a lot to think about. Could he be experiencing some form of power that this world had and our world didn't? That would explain how he'd known there was a cave not far from where we'd originally stopped and that that creature—whatever it was—was nearby.

"A sittack!" Shandry exclaimed when she saw it. She gaped for a moment, as if in shock. "I don't believe it." Her voice was scarcely more than a whisper.

"What?" said Traz, his proud expression faltering a little.

"Those are … " Shandry swallowed, "well, they're practically impossible to catch. Most hunters only dream of catching one. How did you … ?"

"Well," he said in a drawn-out way, "I just sort of knew it was there. So I moved quietly, saw it in the trees, and I slingshot it."

"You brought down a sittack with just a sling?!" Shandry exclaimed. "That's … that's … unheard of! If I didn't know you had to be telling the truth, I'd never believe it."

"Well, then maybe you'll believe me when I tell you there's a cave less than half an hour from here."

Shandry looked closely at Traz, who didn't flinch at her scrutiny. Then she nodded once and turned to kick out the fire. I slung the packs back onto Dyster and untied his reins, then led him along behind the others.

We trudged through the trees to the cave. It was dark before we got there, and, worse, it began to rain. Luckily, there was a lot of dead wood all around, and we had a fire blazing in no time. I hobbled the pony in the back of the cave, took off the packs, and filled his nosebag with grain and some oats. Shandry gathered more wood for the night while Traz dressed the sittack and set it to roast.

I wanted to ask Shandry about the creature—what it was and why it was so hard to catch one—but she seemed to have closed in on herself. Her thoughts were obviously far away.

When the meal was ready, we joined Traz next to the fire. The meat was tender and juicy. At first Shandry seemed reluctant to try it, but Traz held out her plate insistently, so she shrugged and began to eat. There was also flatbread with leten and some kind of root vegetable, yellowy-orange in color and roasted into sweetness.

As we sat around the fire after we'd finished eating, Shandry stroked the pelt of the sittack, which Traz had decided to keep.

"It seems strange," she said, "that the first time I ever see one, it's dead, and then I eat it."

"What's wrong with eating it?" Traz asked.

Shandry shook her head. "Nothing. It's just that the sittack is rather a legendary beast." There was a long pause, and I had to bite my lower lip to keep from demanding more information. "Not just anyone can bring one down. Only special people." A startled look crossed Traz's face. "Only sages. Or so they say."

Traz froze for a moment. Then he drew a deep breath and licked his lips. "Are you saying that *I'm* a sage?"

✦

Many long ages ago, before even history began, night was always black and chill. Folk huddled together and passed the dark time in terror and death, grateful when the grey light of morning banished the darkness.

Boca, however, told stories to her children to stave off their fears. Tales of their father's hunts, brave and true. Tales, funny ones these, of a family of rodents whose escapades left the children in gales of laughter. Tales of love, strong and pure, that never died.

Then Merot, Lord of the Night, heard laughter breaking the silence of the dark. Curious, he came down from the night sky and sat outside Boca's cave, listening to her sweet voice, absent of all fear, spinning its tales to comfort her children.

And he was well-pleased.

And he returned the next night.

And the night after.

A week of nights passed in this way, until Merot decided to reward Boca for the joy she instilled in his breast. In the pink hour after sunset, in that time of light and darkness intertwined when the Lord of the Night may greet the Lady of the Day, Merot asked Willa for a tiny piece of the sun, that he might gift a deserving woman.

And that night, as Boca gathered her children close

around her, a yellow gleam shone in the darkness.
Thus came the light and warmth of fire into the world.

~ an ancient tale from the deeps of time

SEVEN

Shandry shrugged. "How should I know if you're a sage? Maybe that old story is just a legend." She turned her attention back to the sittack pelt, completely unaware of the storm she'd unleashed in our companion.

He sat there unmoving, but I could feel his excitement as if it were water filling the cave and drowning us. A fierce sense of longing, deep wonder, and terrible fear, all churned in and around the small boy who stared into the flames. I put a hand on his shoulder and felt the tension that coursed through him; my hand seemed to grow warm from the contact.

Could it be true? And if it were, what did it mean? The possibilities danced in my mind.

Traz eventually rose to his feet, went beyond the firelight into the cave, and, wrapping himself in his cloak, lay down.

I took the first watch. Long after Shandry's breathing settled into the regular rhythm of sleep, Traz's eyes still glittered in the firelight.

When I began to feel drowsy, I stood up and stepped to the mouth of the cave. Rain poured down in sheets, and I was glad that Traz had found the cave and led us here. Sleeping outside in a deluge like this would've been impossible. With a sigh, I wondered how muddy the road would be now. Shandry was right that we couldn't really have put the journey off, not with Xyla in the condition she was in. But I wished for better weather all the same. We couldn't count on finding a cave every night.

The falling rain had a hypnotic effect on me. The thread of my thought wound its way back to Grey.

A sound from behind startled me. Traz crouched next to the fire, putting more wood on. I went over to him.

"Go ahead and get some sleep," he said. "I can't get any. It's probably time for my watch, anyway."

"I was going to stay up through your turn. You seem too … distracted. Why don't you lie down again?"

"I'm telling you, Donavah, I can't sleep. So you might as well."

"Are you all right?"

He smiled up at me. "Yes, I am. Really and truly. I just want to think about some things. So I might as well watch, if I'm going to be awake anyway."

I was tired, so he didn't have to argue more than that. "All right. But if you get tired before Shandry's watch, wake me."

+ + +

I woke up to see Traz's form silhouetted against heavy snowfall outside. Shandry was lying nearby, also just beginning to stir.

I got up and moved to the fire, grateful to find that Traz had water already heating. A few moments later, Shandry came and joined me by the fire, holding her hands close to the flames and stamping her feet. Traz turned around.

"I'm thinking," he said with a cockeyed grin, "that we're not leaving right away."

Shandry replied, "I hate to get a late start, but I don't think we have any choice."

I stifled a sigh of relief and set about making tea for the three of us while Shandry fed Dyster. I didn't like the idea of delay, either, but surely we couldn't travel until the snow lessened. After handing Shandry and Traz their mugs, I started a pot of porridge.

When we finished eating, I suggested to Traz that he try to get at least a little rest before we left. He lay down and even closed his eyes, but I doubted he slept.

I washed the breakfast things, then made more tea for Shandry and me. No less uneasy than Traz, she paced back and forth between the fire and the cave mouth, until I thought her incessant activity would make me scream. I understood her anxiety about being stuck here, but didn't see how watching the snow would make it go away.

When it finally did stop falling after a little more than an hour, she stepped out without even putting on a cloak and looked up at the sky. She came in a few minutes later, slapping her arms and stamping her feet.

"Brr! It's bitter out there," Shandry said, "but we should probably get going. It looks to stay clear, at least for awhile."

"At least for awhile?" I asked. "What's that supposed to mean? We're not going to leave here, just to get caught with no shelter a few hours from now, are we?"

Shandry made a non-committal sound. "I can't tell what's coming over the mountains. But there's no point in staying here. You know that as well as I do."

She got Traz up and moving while I put the fire out.

Shandry and Traz loaded the packs onto the pony, then we bundled ourselves into our cloaks, hats, and gloves, and filed out of the cave.

Traz led the way back to the road. It didn't seem natural, the way he could lead us so unerringly when he'd never been here before. But as if the incident with the sittack changed everything, Shandry seemed inclined to accept whatever Traz said.

We traveled slowly that day, even once we were back on the road. It didn't snow again, and when the sun cleared the mountaintops ahead of us, it shone enough to take the sting out of the chill. Still, the icy layer under the fresh-fallen snow made for treacherous footing, and each of us fell several times. At least Dyster was sure-footed. Even Traz had to pay attention to where he stepped and resorted to using his staff as a walking stick.

That night and the next were miserable. Traz found us reasonably sheltered places in which to camp, but no more luck finding caves so it was impossible to sleep warmly.

The middle of the fourth day found us crossing over the pass. Not that I would've been able to tell if Shandry hadn't said something. I'd expected the climb to grow steeper as we went higher, but it wasn't like that at all, just a steady rise that eventually flattened out.

"Well," Shandry said, breaking the silence in which we typically walked. "Here we are."

Traz gave her a quizzical look. *"Where* are we?" My question exactly.

"The top. It's not quite all downhill from here, but pretty much."

I let out a snort. "Very funny. We can't be at the top. There are the mountaintops there." I pointed to several peaks on either side of us.

It was Shandry's turn to laugh. "You don't think the road would cross the highest peaks, do you? When there's a pass as low as this?"

I felt myself blush. Of course, now that she pointed it out, it was obvious. Feeling a little stupid, I smiled at her and shrugged.

"It'll be much easier going now. This pass widens into a valley that we can follow pretty much straight down."

Soon we came to a huge meadow. It must be three miles to the other side, I guessed. The wind blew viciously across it, straight into our faces.

"Let's get moving," I said, hunching my shoulders and moving closer to Dyster to try to gain some warmth from his body heat. I was so tired of being cold, and I couldn't wait to get to Delaron. I clucked the pony into motion.

Then I wondered—could I use my maejic to warm myself? Mages used their power to extend the growing season, so why not? It didn't require much thought to keep hold of Dyster's reins and follow the others, so I turned my concentration inward. Imagining a blazing fire on a hearth or a bed piled high with furs didn't work, but just as when I'd tried walking quietly, once I stopped tying to direct the maejic power and just let it flow, it turned to that which I desired. It didn't warm me completely, but it took the edge off the cold, and I was much more comfortable after that.

I tired more quickly that day than ever before. As I sat

next to the fire Traz built, hardly able to keep my eyes open, I wondered what was wrong. The day hadn't been more difficult than any other; as a matter of fact, the terrain was the easiest we'd yet traversed.

Then I realized that, of course, I'd been using my maejic all day. I couldn't remember ever having done that before. Muttering something about needing to meditate, I dug my kit out of my pack and stumbled a short way away. I chose the forest green candle for strength and pale green for health, and settled into the routine.

At first, I was so tired that I found it difficult to keep my mind on what I was doing. Pushing through just drained me further. But as I made myself do it, energy began to seep into me, slowly filling me, renewing my spirit, refreshing my soul. My breathing slowed, as did my heartbeat. I relaxed and centered myself in the inflow of power.

When I finally opened my eyes again and blew out the candles, I felt energized, as if I could run at full speed all the way to Delaron.

+ + +

The next morning, I discovered one big advantage to being on the eastern side of the mountains: the sun shone on us much earlier. Of course, when I remarked on this to Shandry, she pointed out the converse, that we'd lose it earlier in the afternoon, too. That really didn't seem such a huge price to pay for feeling ever so slightly warmer in the morning.

I used my maejic a little more carefully, or maybe the weather was warming up a bit. I was more disciplined than ever about meditating each morning before we left and each afternoon when we stopped, and I tried not to expend any more power than necessary to keep myself comfortable.

Traz had been much quieter than normal ever since that first night, as if the possibility that he was a sage had overtaken all his thoughts. He'd kept to himself, mostly preferring to walk behind us rather than in front. He often seemed lost in thought, pensive and subdued.

The morning of the third day of our descent—a full week now since we'd set out—it rained hard for hours, soaking us all to the skin. At midday, the sun finally came out and warmed us up a little, but the road was slushy underfoot.

In the afternoon, we reached a place that Shandry called "the bends." We'd been descending a great valley, just as Shandry had said. But here, it was as if a knife had sliced a chunk from the mountainside. Where we stood, we looked down a steep hill, down which the road went in tight switchbacks. The hillside was bare of trees, with just an occasional shrub clinging to the sharply angled earth. Far below, the pine forest spread out before us.

Until now, the road had been easy to travel. Shandry said that from late Spring through Autumn, this was a much-used pass, with wagons and carts traversing it easily. During the Winter, though, a better pass farther to the south was the primary trade route. And this part of the road was why. Just that morning's rain had left the footing treacherous.

I paid close attention to where I walked, placing one foot carefully and making sure it was planted before taking the next step. The turns were where it was most dangerous due to the odd camber of the roadway.

About halfway down, Shandry, who was leading Dyster, slipped and fell backward with a loud splash of mud. I'd just turned to help her up, when from behind us, there was a short yelp of surprise, followed by a crashing sound. We looked back just in time to see Traz sliding down the hillside. The slippery slope accelerated his fall, and the road just below barely slowed him at all. He slid out of view without another sound.

✦

When the mighty red dragons first arrived—and we can certainly imagine what a surprise that caused—there was great upheaval. Many of them were extremely antagonistic toward humans, though it was not until later, when we learned of the great persecution from which they had fled, that we understood.

Still, there were those among them who were politic enough to treat with the inhabitants here. They negotiated a home with the sages, newly settled at Lake Delaron, which led to the development of that community—a symbiotic relationship between humans and dragons that continues to this day, all these hundreds of years later.

From this we learn that making peace is always preferable to making war. For the dragons, despite all their power, had ultimately to flee from the humans in their world in order to survive. Yet it is with humans that they now reside in harmony, each lending the other unique elements of their power to create a peace that is itself far greater than the sum of its parts.

-from the lecture notes of Tandor

Eight

"Traz!" Shandry and I screamed in unison. I pulled her to her feet and headed toward the place where he'd tumbled down. I couldn't hurry or I'd fall, too, and it took an agonizingly long time to make the twenty or so steps. Being careful not to overbalance, I looked over the edge. Traz's crumpled form lay unmoving on the road below.

Shandry stood next to me, looking down, her face pale. "Do you think he's all right?" she asked. Dyster, impatient to keep moving, stamped a hoof and snorted.

"We won't know until we get down there. Come on."

It took an eternity to get down to the next level. The urge to rush had to give way to the need for caution. But we finally reached him.

I could tell right away that he was still breathing. He lay on his side. Shandry tied the pony's reins to the nearest shrub, then knelt in the mud near Traz's head. She put one hand on his shoulder to steady him in place while she ran the other down his back. I watched her, anxiety making my heart beat hard.

"His back's all right," she finally said, then she repositioned herself to check his skull. I found myself holding my breath until she looked at me and said, "Just a lump or two, nothing worse."

We gingerly turned him onto his back. And then we

found that he hadn't escaped completely unscathed when we saw the ugly angle at which his lower leg lay in relation to where it should be.

"That's bad," Shandry said. "Do you know how…?"

"I've set a few bones, but always under the healing master's watchful eye and never something this bad."

"You're one up on me there. I know the theory, but haven't ever done it myself."

"We'll just have to do the best we can," I said. I looked around, up and down the hillside, but there weren't any sturdy branches. "There's nothing to splint it with."

"Where's his staff?" Shandry said. "It's too long, but it'll work in a pinch."

"Good thinking. Where'd it land, though?"

Shandry spotted it first, halfway down the next bit of slope. "I'll get it," she said. "You check his arms and other leg."

"Be careful. One accident is already one too many."

"You've got that right."

I turned my attention back to Traz. Everything else felt sound, as far as I could tell. I was glad for his sake that he was unconscious, but I was worried, too. His skull might be intact, but that didn't mean he hadn't hurt his head. He was covered head to foot in mud, and had a scrape along his jaw. A few moments later, Shandry was back.

"What do we do?" she asked, placing the staff on the ground.

"Well, you hold his thigh in place, and I'll straighten his leg."

She crouched down. "I'm awfully glad he's not awake."

I just nodded, trying to summon the courage to do what had to be done.

Shandry took hold of his thigh and gave me a nod. I took his lower leg in both hands and tried to ease it gently into place. It didn't move. I took a deep breath, swallowed, and applied more pressure. Still nothing. Breaking out into a sweat of worry, I closed my eyes and reached for my maejic. I imagined Traz's leg set to rights, and applied even more pressure, gently but steadily. His leg finally moved. When it was straight, someone cried out, and I didn't know whether it was Traz or me. With another nod to Shandry, I let go and wiped the sweat from my brow. Shandry picked up the staff and positioned it while I dug rope out of one of the packs. We bound his leg securely, but not too tightly, and I breathed a sigh of relief. Only to realize that we weren't anything like out of trouble yet.

We were only halfway down the bends, and the footing was bad, but we couldn't stay where we were since there was no shelter or wood for a fire.

"The first way station is at the bottom," Shandry said. "But it's not going to be easy getting him down there."

She'd told us that the folk on this side of the mountain kept way stations for travelers. During the Summer, they'd each be manned with a cook and several other people to help manage things, and traders would set up to supply travelers with food and wares. The rest of the time, no one manned the way stations, but it was expected that anyone staying in one replenished the wood they used.

"This is really *not* good," Shandry said again.

"We'd better just put him on Dyster and hope that he doesn't come to on the way."

I kept a hand on Traz's shoulder, willing him to stay unconscious for now while Shandry rearranged the baggage on the pony. Then, lifting Traz as carefully as we could, we lay him over Dyster's back, his legs dangling down one side and his arms down the other. I could only hope that moving him this way didn't make things worse.

Shandry took the pony's reins while I walked alongside, one hand on Traz's back to keep him from falling off. Dyster, in one of his rare comments, assured me that he understood the importance of not letting the boy fall off.

Going slowly, we made our way down the steep hillside. Though both Shandry and I slipped several times, neither of us fell.

When we got to the bottom, we were both as muddy as Traz. The blood had drained from his face, and he looked to be in a bad way. I wished, as I had a million times on the descent, that he hadn't fallen. Or that I had the power to instantly heal him, though I doubted such a power existed.

"The way station isn't much farther," Shandry said.

Ten minutes later, the most welcome of sights up ahead caught my eyes: a real, proper roof peeked out between the tree trunks. We quickened our steps.

The way station was a large, stone hut, sturdily built and empty of anything except a fireplace and a large store of dry wood. We carried Traz inside and lay him near the hearth. Shandry went back outside to unload Dyster and settle him for the night in the small stable behind the hut. I built a fire and fussed more over Traz. I removed his damp jacket and wrapped him in all the blankets we had with us, then washed the dried mud from his face and hands. I checked his leg and was both relieved and surprised to find that it hadn't swelled up.

By the time Shandry came back inside, the fire had warmed the single room of the hut, and it felt downright luxurious not to feel cold. She let out a sigh of relief as she took off her cloak and hung it next to mine on a peg near the door.

"How is he?" she asked.

"Well, his leg doesn't seem to be any worse, although I don't see how that can be. Not that I'm complaining."

"Let's take it as a good sign."

Traz had hunted well the night before, and we'd packed the extra meat, so I got it out, along with the cooking gear, and started making supper while Shandry took the waterskins out to the well to refill them. I made enough for three, in case Traz awoke, and left his portion in the pot on the edge of the hearth, keeping warm.

After we'd eaten our meal and cleaned the dishes, we sat watching Traz and sipping tea. I wondered how we'd ever complete the journey now.

"Is there somewhere we can take him, where we can find a healer or something?" I asked.

"Not very near," she replied. "A few days' journey on there's ... but, no, we can't go there."

I narrowed my eyes at her. "Where? And why not?"

She didn't answer at first, then shook her head in a slow, almost dreamy way. "The road skirts the edges of his land, and that's too close for comfort as it is."

Before I could ask her who and what she was talking about, a quiet sigh escaped Traz's lips. We both moved nearer to him, but he still didn't show any signs of coming around.

I placed a hand on his chest. His breathing was smooth and regular, his heartbeat strong.

"No fever," Shandry said after feeling his forehead and cheeks. "Not yet anyway."

"I'd feel better if he weren't unconscious," I said, unable to keep the worry out of my voice.

Shandry half-smiled and said, "He wouldn't."

In other circumstances, I would've laughed.

My hand still on Traz's chest, I closed my eyes. The beat of his heart traveled up my arm and into my spirit. It was a strong rhythm, like a large festival drum. My own heart changed its beat to match. As I concentrated on feeling what Traz felt, an unexpected joy welled up inside me, threatening to overflow and break into a dance of celebration.

This couldn't be Traz. Surely his body must be in terrible pain, and not only from his leg, but from his fall, too. Disconcerted, I pulled my hand away and sat there rubbing it.

"What?" Shandry asked in a worried tone.

"Nothing," I said, unsure of what the vision meant and not really wanting to talk about it.

"Is he all right?"

"What do you mean, is he all right?" I exploded. "Of course he's not all right! You know that as well as I do. If there's someplace to go where we can get help, I don't see why you won't tell me."

Her eyes didn't meet mine as she said in a quiet voice, "You just don't understand."

"That's right, I don't understand. I don't understand what could possibly be more important than helping Traz right now. You agreed to lead us, and you were all anxious to leave your old life behind. So if you have a good reason not to help, I'm waiting to hear it."

At first, I didn't think she was going to explain. When she finally began to speak, her voice was low, but it strengthened as she spoke. And this is the story she told me.

When she'd been born, her mother, as was the custom for one who for any reason did not want to raise a child, had left her in the village square, exposed to the elements to die, or to be taken by some pitying soul. Several times each year, the villagers endured the crying of a newborn infant as it lay there, unfed, unloved, unwanted. Winter was more merciful, for usually the babe died in the night.

Shandry, though, disappeared as soon as it grew dark—the first baby in living memory to be taken in. And even more interesting to the village gossips, nobody knew who had taken her. No one had been seen passing through that day or the next, and there were no families with an unaccounted baby. She simply disappeared in the night, never to be seen again.

The old couple who took her were sages, very powerful ones who'd been cast out of their community. They'd raised Shandry as their own, teaching her skills both mundane and arcane, for they knew that she, too, would be outcast and would have to rely on herself for everything. And indeed, they'd died before she was sixteen.

In the two years since, Shandry had grown and hunted her own food, made her own clothes and weapons, and spun and woven her own cloth. She crystal-gazed, scryed, and attuned herself to the earth's life-force.

I didn't interrupt her while she told me all this, and when she stopped speaking, it was several moments before my mind settled on which question to ask first.

"But don't you get lonely, never seeing *anyone?*"

She wiped a sleeve across her nose, just as Traz might if he thought no one was looking. "I didn't before Ama and Paypa died, and since then, I've had too much to do to be lonely." But she didn't meet my gaze, and I didn't press her.

"Well, what did Ama and Paypa do to get cast out? That sounds pretty serious."

"Depends on your point of view. The eldest son of the local lord was studying at the order house where they taught."

"He was going to become a sage?"

Shandry shook her head. "I don't think so. Rennirt would've had to give up his place in the succession of the lordship if he'd done that. I think his father sent him to the order house in hopes he'd acquire some discipline. That's what Ama told me, anyway. But he liked best to use his power to bully other students and even some of the sages. After more warnings than any regular student would've gotten, he finally got involved in some scandal, and my parents, who were the leaders of the order house, forced him to leave."

"A scandal? What kind?"

"I ... I don't really know. Of course, the lord didn't like them doing that to his precious son, so he stirred up the order against them. About six months after they forced Rennirt out, the order forced *them* out."

"So it didn't do them much good in the end, did it?"

"Not really. Except for keeping their integrity. Then the old lord died shortly after that, and Rennirt took his place. He purged the house of anyone who still supported my parents."

"And this Rennirt, his lands are nearby, and it's his healers who are nearest?"

Shandry nodded her head miserably. "The road skirts his lands."

"I still don't see why it's a problem," I said. "No one knows who you are."

She looked straight at me now, fire smoldering behind the tears in her eyes. "You really don't get it, do you?"

"No! I don't!"

"Why can't you just believe me that we don't want to come any closer to that man than possible?"

"Because we're talking about my best friend being hurt!" I was shouting now, not caring about the noise.

Shandry shouted back. "Has it occurred to you that there are more important things?"

"No! No, it hasn't! Because Traz is almost the most important thing in the world to me right now."

"Well, that's your problem, isn't it?"

"It's your problem, too! We're all three stuck here, in case you hadn't noticed." She didn't say anything to that. "So what if this Lord Rennirt is as horrible as you say? What possible difference does it make?"

We stared at one another, tension boiling up between us.

Shandry's jaw worked for a moment, then she finally blurted out, "Because he's my father."

My anger instantly evaporated as her words left me speechless. I felt like I'd just been punched in the stomach. Shandry rose to her feet and left the hut, letting the door slam behind her. I stared at it for a few moments, torn between understanding her reluctance and wanting to get help for Traz.

When it occurred to me that she'd left without putting on her cloak, I went to the door and called out to her. No reply. I put on mine and took hers, then went outside. I called again, but still no answer. It was too dark to go looking for her, but I made a circuit of the hut anyway. She didn't come back, so I went back inside.

I still hadn't resolved the dilemma of what to do when she returned an hour later.

"You must be freezing," I said. "Why don't you wrap up in both our cloaks and get some sleep? I'll take first watch."

Shivering, she nodded.

I took a double watch, thinking she needed the extra rest to get over being chilled. When I woke her to relieve me, it felt good to lie down and fall asleep in a warm room.

I dreamt of Anazian. Watching me. Laughing at me. My mouth was dry, and I felt thirsty deep in my soul. Oh, so thirsty. A rattling noise, and then something shook me, hard, as if to tear my flesh from my bones.

But, of course, it was only Shandry shaking me. It must be time for my next watch. The dream had been disturbing, and I didn't feel at all rested as I sat up.

"Sorry to wake you so soon, but it's Traz," she said. "He's mumbling in his sleep."

I scooted over to him. His lips moved, and random, unintelligible sounds came from his mouth. His voice grew louder and stronger, as if it were getting used to speaking aloud again after a long silence, but the words were no more distinguishable than before.

Then, without any warning, his eyes flew open and he sat up. If his leg hadn't been immobile, bound to his staff, I was sure he would've sprung to his feet.

"What?" he cried out. "Where? Who?"

✦

I am trapped like an animal in a cage. I pace round and round in an endless circle. To my surprise, I find I'm crawling on all fours. Have I become an animal? Tears stream down my face, and I lick them, their saltiness filling my mouth and increasing my thirst.

"We have only just begun," says a voice nearby. Is he speaking to me? Of me? My thoughts are vague and dim. "All will be well, and you will learn the error of your ways. Then we shall dance together with joy. You will see."

But I cannot dance; I cannot even stand. I can only pace. Round and round and round I go as that which makes me human flees.

Nine

I put a hand on Traz's shoulder, trying to convey a sense of calm to his spirit. His eyes lost a little of their wildness.

"Donavah?" he said, peering at me. "Is that really you? I thought ... but no, that must've been a dream." He rubbed his face. "What happened? Where are we?"

Shandry went to Traz's other side and handed him a steaming cup. "Here. Drink this. You need it more than I do."

Traz took the cup and sniffed it, then sipped. "I still don't understand. Where are we? What is this place?" He made a move as if trying to stand. "And why is my staff tied to my leg?"

We told him what had happened.

"But," he said with a frown when we'd finished, "I feel fine. My leg doesn't hurt at all."

I examined it again. It did indeed feel perfectly normal. But even if we'd managed to set it properly, Traz should still be in a great deal of pain. "Well, I'll take the splint off," I said. "I can check it over better that way, anyway. But if it hurts, you tell me immediately."

"Don't worry, I'll shout." And his impudent grin flashed in the firelight. If I hadn't known better, I'd never have believed he'd just awakened from almost a full day of being unconscious.

Shandry and I worked together to unbind Traz's leg. We

went slowly and carefully. About the time we reached his knee, Traz winced loudly. We both froze until he started giggling. I swatted his arm, then went back to work.

"Now, don't bend it," I said when we'd finished. "Just sit there until I say." I felt his leg, paying special attention to his knee, but as before, nothing at all seemed wrong. "Are you sure it doesn't hurt?"

"Why would I lie about something like that? Now would you please just let me get up? I'm kind of stiff, you know."

Shandry and I shared a confused look. "Start by trying to bend your knee," I said.

He drew both legs up to his chest. "There. Are you satisfied?" And before either Shandry or I could say anything more, he rose to his feet and started walking around the hut. He stretched out his arms and swung them around, then raised them high over his head. I could almost feel his spine pop.

Still sitting facing me, Shandry whispered, "It's not possible. It's just not possible."

I agreed, but still hadn't found my voice with which to express it.

Traz came back to the fire, picked up the cup of tea, and drank some more. "Now," he said, "is there anything to eat in this place? I'll cook it myself if you two are just going to stare at me like a couple of noodges."

I almost burst out laughing.

+ + +

The next few days we made good progress. The weather held reasonably fine, the hunting was good, and we hadn't come close to running out of supplies. Every day, I got better and better at husbanding the use of my maejic so that I stayed comfortable but didn't use too much, and each afternoon's meditation refilled me. Traz went on as he'd started, walking ahead of us twirling his staff in ever more complicated patterns, and now I didn't begrudge a moment of it.

Shandry and I never talked about the argument we'd had and the revelations she'd shared. I felt uncomfortable knowing these intimate things about her life and wished I could just forget them. She, in turn, grew distant from me, as if she wished she hadn't spoken up, especially as events turned out.

Three days after Traz's accident, we passed a stone marker. The four-sided obelisk stood about waist high, and on each face, carved in relief, was a dragon whose impossibly long tail swirled into complex curlicues. The design somehow tricked the eye, making it appear as if the dragons were in motion.

Shandry stood in the middle of the road, arms crossed over her chest and a closed expression on her face, while Traz and I examined the marker, laughing in fascination at the illusion.

"C'mere and look at this," Traz said, trying to coax some interest out of Shandry. "It's just about the most amazing thing I've ever seen."

She gave a stiff shake of her head. "I don't need to see it." Her words came out tight and clipped. "I know what it is."

I looked at her closely and asked, "And that would be?"

"Can't you guess?" Her eyes were black as well as bleak.

"I've never seen anything like it before. What is it?"

She let out a hiss of exasperation. "It's the marker for Rennirt's lands. Now, can we please get moving? It's three days to the other marker, and the sooner we get there, the better."

Traz scowled at me in frustration when I agreed with Shandry that we should be going. I could only hope he wouldn't question me about it later. I didn't want to lie to him, but I couldn't tell him Shandry's secrets, either.

We didn't come to the next way station until well after dark. When the sun set, Traz complained and said it was warm enough to camp, but though he was right about that, Shandry and I both wanted to push on.

When we finally reached the way station, we followed our usual routine. Shandry unloaded and stabled Dyster, I gathered more wood so we wouldn't have to do it in the morning, and Traz started cooking the meal. Shandry hadn't wanted to let Traz out of sight in the afternoon, which is when he'd typically do the hunting for our supper, so we had to settle for porridge. Traz started to complain again, but I quelled him with a look. Shandry was taut with tension, and I was afraid she might come completely undone at any moment.

After the meal, I went into a corner, which was as much privacy as I could get in the way stations, to meditate.

At first, it had been hard to meditate in such close proximity to others, but I was growing accustomed to it. I slid through the steps easily this time. I'd not used much maejic during the day, so wasn't in need of refilling. Instead, my spirit soared through the openness of the ether where lights of every color shot like falling stars across the sky. A warming sense of welcome enclosed me like a mother's embrace.

"What have we here? Well met again, indeed."

The words, spoken in that same quiet, melodious voice as before, froze my blood. And as before, I didn't reply.

There was a soft gasp of sharply drawn breath, then, "Ride like the wind!"

Everything went black, and I fell to earth.

I came to myself with a bit of a start. I blew out the candles but remained sitting where I was. Pondering. I'd been so sure that it had been Shandry back on that first day. After all, she'd admitted that she'd been seeking me, and I hadn't encountered that presence while meditating since then. I glanced surreptitiously over a shoulder to see what she was doing, only to find her engaged with Traz in a quiet conversation. Just as they usually did while I meditated. It didn't make any sense. For the first time since arriving on Stychs, I missed Yallick. Surely he would've been able to explain what these strange meditation sessions meant.

Eventually, unable to make any sense of what had happened, I put my meditation kit away. I felt sleepy and yawned.

Shandry said, "I have first watch tonight. If you're that tired, why don't you go to sleep?"

"I think I will," I said with another huge yawn.

I rolled up in my cloak, and the crackling of the fire and the soft voices of the others sent me to sleep.

+ + +

Later that night, it seemed as if I'd scarcely fallen back to sleep after my watch when I was awakened by the door of the hut slamming against the wall, followed by a rush of people inside. I sat up, blinking my eyes in the dim light of the low fire. Beside me, Traz was doing the same.

Someone shouted, "Don't move!" and kicked Traz in the ribs.

Before I could move a muscle, someone else swept into the hut, bowing his head so as not to strike it on the door frame. Fear spread out from this man, filling the room like a black fog and gripping my heart. I shrank back, wishing there were something to hide behind.

His presence reeked of power; I could practically taste it, and its flavor was sour and rancid. I tried to get my breath as magic used up the air in the room.

Traz let out a moan and vomited, drawing the attention of the man, who stooped over him and prodded him with a toe.

"Ah, interesting." The man dragged a finger across Traz's brow. Traz cried out in pain, and I scrambled to his side. The man held up a hand, freezing me in place. He looked through my eyes and straight into my soul.

I couldn't breathe. My heart stopped beating. I closed my eyes, struggling against panic. My thoughts grew cloudy. Then he released me, and I fell to the ground before him, gasping for breath.

"This one," he said, pointing a long finger at me, and this time, I recognized his strong, melodious voice.

Hands grabbed me, lifting me to my feet. The man took my chin in his hand and forced my face upward. With his other hand, he traced my lips with a finger. Something tightened in my throat. He passed his thumbs over my eyes, and everything went completely black. I cried out in surprise, but no sound came out. He chuckled.

"And something to keep you from using all that luscious power. Open your mouth."

I wanted to resist. I intended to. But as if I were being controlled by someone or something other than my own will, my lips parted and my mouth opened.

Something hard and round was shoved in. It had a bitter flavor that made me gag and try to spit it out.

"Now, none of that," said the man, and a moment later a strip of cloth was wound around the lower part of my face. "I leave her to you, now. I shall expect you before sundown tomorrow."

With an evil laugh, the man stepped away. A moment later, he and his magic were gone.

✦

When Oggam learnt that his daughter, Dayrina was with child, he was livid. For Dayrina—his only offspring—had no husband, nor would she tell him who the father was.

Oggam went to the herb woman and demanded she make the strongest abortifacient possible. The herb woman objected that the efficacy of the potion was related directly to the desire of the one who consumed it, but Oggam was not to be gainsaid.

He forced Dayrina, who was all unwilling, to drink deeply of the potion. When days and days passed with no sign of miscarriage, Oggam grew angrier than ever.

He tried other methods, grim and cruel, to loose the baby from Dayrina's womb, but to no avail. Dayrina held fast to the soul who grew within her, and in the fullness of her time, she brought forth a healthy baby son, bearing the same clover-leaf birthmark on his shoulder that Dayrina had and as had her mother before her.

Oggam, however, took the babe and, locking Dayrina in the pantry, took him to the village green, leaving him in the appointed spot to die or be taken, howsoever it was meant to be.

Dayrina beat upon the door, pleading with her father not to do this thing. She worked to loose the hinges until her fingers bled. But Oggam's heart would not be softened toward her, this daughter of his old age, this girl who reminded him in so many ways of her long-dead mother.

The next afternoon, a village elder arrived with the news that the baby had been taken, no one knew by whom. Oggam sighed in relief while Dayrina wept for sorrow.

Not wanting to risk another unwanted grandchild, Oggam sold the house and removed far away, to a distant village where he had kin. Surely now life would return to its former happy routine.

But Dayrina pined for her lost son. By rights, the day he turned six months old should have been his naming day. Then his first birthday, which should have been a day of celebration, passed. But Dayrina did not recover from her grief as these anniversaries passed, and on the eve of her son's second birthday, she died of a broken heart.

Finally, belatedly, Oggam grasped the error of his chosen way. He wept at Dayrina's grave, beating his hands on the earth and tearing out his hair. When the worst of his grief had burnt itself out, he resolved to right what he had done wrong: he would find Dayrina's son and bring him up himself. Let the child take his mother's place as Oggam's heir, that his despair might be relieved and his line not come to an end.

He returned to his village and began to seek in earnest. Word went far and wide that Oggam sought the child who'd been taken from the village green two years before. But every clue he chased, every faint path of hope he followed, all came to naught.

Then one night a dark figure came to his door. Oggam could not tell whether it was a man or a woman, neither by *appearance nor by voice. This person, who claimed no name other than "wise one," would not set foot across the doorstep, but from the shadows offered to find Oggam's grandson. It would take, promised the wise one, nothing more than a simple ritual of finding, one that was known to only a few. The cost: everything that Oggam had—his gold, his property, all that he valued. And yet all this, set against keeping his name alive, was as nothing to Oggam, who willingly agreed to the price.*

As instructed, at midnight nine days later, Oggam arrived at the place the wise one had told him, a secret place deep in the bosom of the mountains, a place of mystery and of magic and of marvel. The black-cloaked wise one stood at the head of a large, flat stone on which lay a covered bundle. Oggam crept nearer, fearful yet curious to see a ritual the like of which he'd never heard of before this.

The wise one muttered words in a language Oggam did not know, whilst candles, magically suspended in the air, flickered. With an unexpected movement, the wise one whisked off the covering from the bundle to reveal a small human figure bound to the stone, gagged and unmoving. Oggam recoiled from the sight but felt compelled to keep watching, anxious that this ritual of finding succeed.

With an unearthly cry, the figure raised a knife above the stone. Its blade glittered in the moonlight, capturing a beam and reflecting it onto the figure below.

In which Oggam saw, only a second before the knife plunged into the child's heart, Dayrina's clover birthmark.

~an ancient tale from the deeps of time

Ten

Before I could gather my wits, a woman with a sharp, nasal voice said, "Tie 'em up."

Moments later, my hands were bound securely behind me.

The woman who'd given the order whispered in my ear, her breath warm and sour on my cheek. "Rennirt is well pleased. Oh, yes, very well pleased indeed."

Rennirt! Shandry's father!

"Shove them off into the corners. And make sure they can't move."

The guards holding me dragged me to a corner and forced me facedown to the ground. They tied my ankles together, then, to my horror, pulled them up behind me and tied them to my wrists. My leg muscles cramped up against the awkward position and tears sprang to my eyes.

In a miasma of fear and pain, I lay there, unable to do anything—not even move—except listen to the guards' long carousing. From their voices, I concluded they were all women. The sound and the smell of them filled the room.

I couldn't tell if the thing in my mouth was a stone of some kind, or perhaps the pit of a strange fruit, or what. It no longer tasted horrible; it had no flavor at all for it had numbed my tongue. Swallowing was making my throat grow numb, too. Stranger than that, though, was the numbness that blanketed my maejic. Anazian had cast a spell on me that made me believe I'd lost my power, so I knew that feeling well. But this was different from that time.

I withdrew deep into myself. The laughter and bawdy conversation of the women became so much sighing of wind in trees. I couldn't be bothered to give a drop of attention to it.

I sought my maejic. When at first I couldn't find it, I tried not to panic. Anazian, for all the effort he'd put into trying, hadn't been able to take it away; surely neither could Rennirt. I must simply go deeper to find it. I slowed my breathing, calmed the beat of my heart. Being unable to move or to see seemed to help, to strengthen my inward focus.

And there it was, so deep in my soul I almost missed it. It was hard and cold, like a lump of ice. I touched it, gingerly, not wanting to damage it. It burned like fire yet left frostbite behind. Its heart was still aflame, just waiting to be loosened. Once the stone was out of my mouth, I knew my maejic would burst forth into life again. I need only be patient.

When my awareness of my surroundings returned, all I could hear was the crackling and snapping of the flames in the fireplace. Our guards must be asleep now. From outside came sounds of snuffling and the occasional stamp of horses' hoofs. Inside, I identified six distinct breathing patterns: four slept, one was awake and alert—that must be the watch— and one shallow and labored: Traz.

I wanted to sleep, but the discomfort was too great. My shoulders and thighs ached, while I lost the feeling in my fingers, ears, and nose.

Then someone was fumbling with my bindings, and the

jerks and tugs sent spasms of agony through my body. I must finally have dozed off, and I could have wished for a kinder awakening.

The tension on my legs eased. I tried to straighten them, but could barely move. Two of the women pulled me to my feet, but my legs couldn't take the sudden strain and I collapsed right back down. My head cracked painfully on the floor.

"Oh, just carry her," came the sharp command from the leader.

"Shall I give her some water?" asked a voice next to me.

The leader snorted. "A day without water isn't going to be killing anyone."

One of my captors shoved a shoulder into my stomach and lifted me. As she carried me away, colors that seemed to emanate from where my head had struck the floor flashed across the insides of my eyelids with each step.

Outside, she dumped me on the ground. After forcing me into a sitting position, she untied my hands from behind my back and retied them in front of me.

"I suppose you'll be needing to relieve yourself. And you'd better, because I'm not wanting to smell your stink later." She tugged down my trousers, and when I was finished, pulled them up again.

Then, with no more regard than if I were a sack of grain, she picked me up and tossed me across an unsaddled horse, my legs dangling down one side, my head and arms down the other. Just like Traz a few days ago, except, of course, that I was conscious. Another guard helped her to secure me in place with a harness while the others saddled the remaining horses.

The blood rushed to my head and I had to suppress the urge to vomit.

Someone shouted that breakfast was ready, and I was left to worry what would happen next, how long the ordeal ahead would last, and how badly they'd hurt Traz.

The meal seemed to drag on; with no points of reference, I couldn't really tell the passage of time. I was all alone in my uncomfortable little world. The horse stamped impatiently several times, sending shudders through my frame.

After an interminable time, the guards came out, joking and laughing. They mounted up, and we all began to move. Each step sent a judder of pain through me. When, once the horses were warmed up for their day's exercise, the leader sang out the order to trot, I wanted to scream. Instead, I passed out.

+ + +

All day, I slipped in and out of consciousness. Each awakening was worse than the one before. My bones screamed in agony, my muscles froze into knots, and my tendons burned. But worst of all was the thirst. My lips felt cracked, and I was sure they must be bleeding. My whole body ached for water.

Early on, though I knew it would be useless, I tried to speak with the horse. If only I could make enough contact to get it to smooth its gait. That alone would be a triumph. Alas, the stone did exactly the job it was meant to.

The group stopped for the midday meal. Before we started again, one of the women tested the straps holding me to the horse, but she needn't have bothered. I hadn't moved an inch on the first part of the journey, and I doubted I'd ever move again.

The afternoon lasted an eternity. When I was conscious, I turned all my attention in on myself, trying to strengthen my body to withstand this ordeal, trying to ignore where the straps seemed to be cutting into my flesh. I focused my mind on transcending the pain. This would surely be over some day, and when that day arrived, I wanted to be strong—in mind, if not in body—to face whatever came next.

Then finally, after twenty lifetimes, it was over. The women called out and were answered by male voices. The women's voices went off in one direction while my horse was led in another. My feet crashed painfully against something, which I concluded was a doorframe when the air changed from feeling open and chill to being enclosed and warm. I guessed it must be a stable.

Several pairs of hands loosed me from the horse. They slid me off one side and I fell in a heap, unable to stand or even to move.

"All right, then," a loud male voice said, hurting my ears, "I'm not supposing you can walk." He laughed at his own joke. "I guess I'll be having to carry you."

He picked me up as if I weighed nothing and tossed me over his shoulder. Someone made weak little groaning noises with every step the man took, and I realized it was me.

Out into the open again, then back indoors. His footsteps rang out on a stone floor. After a little while, he stopped. Another man made a strange grunting noise, then I heard a metallic rattle, a loud click, and the creak of door hinges.

The man carrying me stepped through and, as the door closed and locked behind us, began descending a staircase that went on and on, turn after turn, forever.

We finally stopped at what must be the bottom. Another voice made a series of unintelligible grunts, after which the man carried me a little farther. More key rattling, another lock turning, and a door scraped open. I was dumped onto a damp stone floor. The man untied my wrists, making me want to weep for joy, only to secure them behind me again.

"That'll be doing you for awhile," he said. The door closed, the lock clicked into place, and I was all alone.

I didn't even try to move; I just lay there like a dead thing. I'd been without eyesight for almost a full day now, and my hearing had grown keen when I cared to listen. I did now, but heard nothing—no footsteps, no keys, no locks, no doors. Was there simply no noise beyond the door, or was it so heavy that it blocked outside sound?

My thoughts twisted in on themselves, and as time crept past, my imagination began to supply the sensory stimulation that was lacking. Colors swirled before my eyes, resolving into images then dissolving into haze. A mountain reflected perfectly in a still lake. Sunset beyond a field of ripened wheat. Water trickling over stones in a creek. And I even heard the babble, which, as I tried to force my mind away from water, turned into a distant chanting. I strained my ears to catch the words, sure that they would supply the magic to free me.

My senses threatened to take me on a hallucinatory ride, and there was nothing I could do to prevent it. I could only hope that my sanity would be intact on the other side.

But then a sound—a real sound—chased the imaginary ones away. The door was opening. I lay still, hoping they would think me asleep. Footsteps approached, and someone crouched down next to me. My heart pounded so hard that it sent flashes of light into my brain.

The person held a cloth over my nose.

At this new threat, my body burst into life. I struggled in earnest, not wanting to die, not now, not here, not this way. As I tried to draw air into my lungs, a pungent odor filled my nostrils, unfamiliar, but not unpleasant. Still, I jerked my head from side to side, but it was no difficult thing for the person to keep the cloth over my nose.

My body began to relax, loosen up, float away. I released my consciousness to follow.

✦

Dear Botellin~

As requested, I'm writing to let you know how things progress with young Xyla.

I'm pleased to report that she does exceedingly well. She fits in with the other younglings as if she were one of their clutch-mates. Indeed, they were all so young when she came to us that I think they have forgotten she is not one of them.

She has not yet explained why she came, beyond saying there was need of her to "grow." We have not been able to get anything more out of her on that topic.

You asked about her power, and all I can say is that it is very great. But then, we already knew that, for one as young as she to make the jump between the worlds. To come near her is to sense her power lying hidden just beneath the surface.

In the meantime, she brings us all great pleasure.

~Until our next,
Falana, Sage

Eleven

I awoke to find myself strapped securely and uncomfortably to a heavy wooden chair. As I grew more aware of my body, I found that I could scarcely move more than my head, with straps at my ankles, knees, waist, elbows, and wrists.

Someone was in the room: I could feel the power of their presence. A rustling sound directly behind me. Then a soft touch on my eyelids, and I could see again.

In front of me was a table and an empty chair. On the table sat a pitcher and glass, several fine tools I didn't recognize, some small pots, and a single lit candle, beyond the light of which all was darkness. The candlelight hurt my eyes.

"Ah, yes. Yes," said a quiet male voice, smooth and rich. Rennirt. "I feel you burn."

From behind, two hands were placed on my head. The fingertips, positioned seemingly with care, were cool and refreshing. They quenched the fire in my soul.

"You will submit to my power. All do, sooner or later." The voice coated my raw nerves like honey. I wanted to cooperate, to please this man, to give him what he wanted.

His hands moved, and the next thing I knew he was untying the linen strips that bound my mouth. Tenderly, tenderly, he unwound the cloth. Whenever his skin touched mine, a thrill went through me. Then the hateful cloth was gone, but my jaw was stiff, and it was those gentle fingers that removed the stone.

I took great gulps of air. The relief of the release was so intense I began to sob.

"There, there. It's all right." The hands stroked my cheeks, my forehead, my hair, comforting me. "You needn't weep. You just had to be taught."

I wanted to speak, to ask what he wanted me to learn and why I needed to be taught in such harsh fashion. But my tongue was like a block of wood in my mouth, nor would my lips move.

He must have sensed my desire, for his next words were, "No, you will not speak until I say you may. Disobedience will bring punishment, not merely instruction."

And under the influence of his voice, this seemed reasonable to me.

Now my eyes caught sight again of the pitcher, and thirst overcame me. I tried to reach for the glass, only for my restraints to remind me that I couldn't.

Finally, Rennirt came around to where I could see him.

He was tall and slender and beautiful. He wore dark clothes and a rich blue over-robe shot with gold thread. His hair, black and straight, fell past his waist. His skin was even darker than Shandry's. But his face drew and held my attention. He had mobile, expressive lips, high cheekbones, and a thin, fine nose. His eyes were bright green and twinkled in the candlelight.

With graceful moves, like those of a dancer, he sat in the chair across from me, poured water into the glass, and drank.

I wanted to ask—to beg—for a drink, but his eyes held mine, forbidding me from saying a word.

He drank again, his Adam's apple bobbing as he swallowed. He emptied the glass, and refilled it. "I want to understand your power," he said, as if he were asking me something as simple as how to tie a knot. He drank again. I couldn't take my eyes off the glass as he drank from it. "You will tell me of your power. You will give me your power. And you will be mine."

He set the glass down and clapped his hands together twice.

A door behind me opened and closed, and a moment later a short, dark man came into view. He bowed deferentially. "My lord Rennirt."

"We are ready," Rennirt said, setting down the glass and rising to his feet in a fluid movement. I found I couldn't take my eyes from him, and his lips curved into a satisfied smile. "She's pretty enough, for all her pale skin." He reached out a hand and with a fingertip traced a pattern on my cheek. I shivered at his touch. "The Etosian knot, I think."

The other man nodded. "Very good, my lord."

"Do not worry," Rennirt said to me. "Master Ganwin is a fine artist, as long as you don't move."

My mind, still muddled and slow from the previous day's ordeal, grasped for meaning of these words. Etosian knot? Artist?

Rennirt moved behind my chair again while Ganwin examined the tools on the table, repositioning several. Rennirt took my head in his hands again and turned it to the right, firmly and irresistibly. At a word of command, the room blazed with light from torches on the wall. I blinked my eyes against this new pain.

I felt more than saw Ganwin come near. He brushed my left cheek gently, softly, as tenderly as a mother touching her newborn babe. Something glittered near my eye, and the next thing I knew, he cut into my face.

I gasped. Had it been possible, I would've jerked my head away. But there I was, pinned in place with Rennirt holding fast to my head and now squeezing my skull painfully between his hands.

"I warned you against moving," he said, his voice harsh and bitter now. "Do not think to do so again. If you spoil the design, I will make sure you regret it."

Ganwin made fast work of a number of sweeping curves. Blood ran down, but he wiped it away with a piece of fine cotton. My hands clenched and my muscles tightened in resistance. Stars of yellow pain flashed in my mind, and I almost stopped breathing. If only I could pass out! But even as consciousness began to flee, Rennirt's power drew it back. He actually *wanted* me to feel this pain and would allow no relief.

After the shock of the first few cuts, my face began to go numb, as if my body were reacting to the pain by making me not feel it.

Rennirt said, "Use the silver. Subtle, but clear."

Ganwin picked up one of the several pots that sat on the table. He opened it where I could see, and it contained a shimmery powder that glinted where the light caught it. With another tool, he inserted the powder into the cuts on my face.

I bit my lower lip to keep from crying out at this new

agony. Bit by bit, he pressed the powder in, while I tried to take deep, relaxing breaths and send my mind far away. When Ganwin set the pot back on the table, I breathed a sigh of relief, only to find him picking up the knife again.

I don't know how long it took to finish the job. When it was finally done, my left cheek burned.

Rennirt let my head go and came around to look at Ganwin's handiwork. I didn't move.

"As beautiful as ever. A masterful job."

"Thank you, my lord."

The small man shuffled away, and again, I heard the door open and close.

Rennirt sat back down, poured himself some more water and drank. "You took that well, all in all," he said.

As if I had a choice, I thought.

And Rennirt laughed. "I suppose you had no choice at all. Now, I rather suspect you're thirsty." He poured more water, leaned across the table, and held the glass to my lips. Had my thirst been less, I might have had the will to refuse, but I gulped the water, grateful for it and shamed by my gratitude.

He let me have only a few mouthfuls, though. "Now, the important thing is that you let it heal properly. The cuts are thin and not very deep, for all that it must feel otherwise. They should heal nicely. If you pick at them, though, the scars will thicken and turn ugly. That would displease me. If I find that you pick at them, I'll have your hands bound behind you until the healing is finished. Do you understand?"

I nodded, and the motion sent fresh waves of pain through me.

Rennirt clapped his hands, and someone entered. "Take her away. And see that she's fed and watered."

Without a word, a large man dressed in a military-looking uniform unbound me from the chair. He gestured toward the door with his head. I looked to Rennirt for permission, and he smiled again in obvious satisfaction. "Begone."

I rose cautiously to my feet. Lightheadedness forced me to move slowly. The guard led me to the door, held it open to let me pass through, then led me on. It was a long way, or at least it seemed so to me. Another guard opened a door and locked it behind us once we passed through. Just beyond was a staircase leading down. I knew now where we were. Tears began to trickle from my eyes. The salt from them stung my left cheek, but I dared not touch that side of my face.

Going down, I tried to count the steps to keep my mind off myself, but I lost count sometime after one hundred. Down, down we went, with nothing but a torch at each turning of the stair to light the way.

There was a last torch at the bottom, where corridors stretched away both right and left. Unlit, it was impossible to tell how far they went. Another guard stood watch. Without a word, he took the torch from its holder, nodded to the left, and gestured for me to follow. The guard who'd brought me here started back up the stairs. We passed a number of cells, and I wondered which one held Traz.

We stopped at a door, which the guard unlocked and pushed open. He shoved me inside. I stood frozen as he shut the door behind me, leaving me in the dark once again.

After awhile, I got down on my hands and knees and

explored the cell. In one corner was a thin layer of straw, in another a bucket. Nothing else but rough-cut stone floor and walls.

As I sat huddled on the straw, there was a strange sliding noise. A faint light gleamed for a moment from the general direction of the door while something was shoved into my cell. Then it went dark again.

I inched forward, feeling my way. On the floor just in front of the door my seeking hands found a chunk of bread, a bit of something rubbery that might be cheese, and, to my intense relief, a metallic cup filled with liquid. I sipped. Yes, it was water. Stale, dank water that I could only hope wouldn't make me ill, but water all the same.

The bread was dry, as I knew it would be, and the cheese had a mildewy flavor. But I had no idea how long it had been since I'd last eaten nor how long before I would eat again, so I ate it all, using care not to drop even a crumb if I could help it. I only sipped at the water, restraining with difficulty the urge to gulp it, wanting to make it last as long as possible.

I dozed after that, but fitfully, aware even in my sleep that I mustn't touch the left side of my face, no matter how much it burned.

Sometime later—how long, I had no way of telling—my cell door opened. The light and sound had a quality of reality that assured me I wasn't dreaming. I sat frozen on my pile of straw, fearing what would happen next.

A young woman slipped in, a basket in one hand and a lighted candle in the other. The door closed behind her, and the lock clicked into place.

"It's all right," she said, her voice soft and gentle, as if she were speaking to a trapped animal. In a way, she was. "I'm here to help you."

I didn't reply but just stared as she set the candle on the floor in the center of the cell. She moved closer to me, and I backed as far into the corner as I could. Who was she, and why was she here? No one that Rennirt would allow to visit me could be trustworthy; of that much, I felt sure.

"I've come to treat your face."

My hand rose instinctively to my cheek though didn't actually touch it. Rennirt's threat to bind my hands had struck deep into my soul. "No." I shook my head. "Don't touch me." My entire body began to shudder.

"I'm not going to hurt you. I've a poultice that will ease some of the burning, and a salve to speed the healing." I shook my head again. "Please, won't you at least let me look at it?"

"Can't exactly stop you, can I?"

She bowed her head slightly, acknowledging the truth of what I said. "No, I don't suppose so. But I'd prefer to have your permission."

I considered, and she waited without moving. "What will you do if I say no?"

She sighed. "Please, just let me do my job. It will be easier for both of us that way."

"What's your job?" I spat the words out. "To bungle the healing so he can torture me more?"

Her eyes closed in a wince, as if my words struck a nerve. "No, truly not." She held out her hand, palms facing me, in entreaty. "Honest told, I am here to help you."

"And why would he—" I refused to speak his name aloud "—wish for anyone to help me?"

"I'm a healer, sworn never to harm but only to heal. Even Lord Rennirt doesn't have the power to make me do otherwise. Here." She took something from the basket and held it out to me. "See for yourself."

I reached out a shaking hand and took what she offered. It was a poultice, warm and damp and fragrant. The scent of it seemed to cleanse the air around me.

"Go ahead," she said, nodding encouragingly. "Apply it to your face."

I felt torn. Rennirt had said not to touch it. Surely he would know if I did. On the other hand, this healer couldn't possibly be here without his knowledge and permission. And in truth, the vibrations I felt from her were nothing but positive. Yet how could I trust her? Perhaps it was a trick. As I sat there, trying to decide what to do, she mimed holding something to her cheek. Almost of its own volition, my hand rose and pressed the poultice to my own cheek. Although it was warm, it instantly quenched the fire that I'd been barely managing to ignore. In relief, my whole body relaxed a little—a very little. I leaned back against the wall and half-closed my eyes. I still didn't trust this woman.

"Ten minutes will do," she said, now busy rummaging in the basket.

With the candlelight mostly behind her, I couldn't tell much about what she looked like, other than having skin lighter than Rennirt's and hair in braids like Shandry's.

"I'm Soola," she said, and somehow hearing her state her

name disposed me ever so slightly more in her favor. I did not, however, return the courtesy. Rennirt hadn't spoken my name yet, and if he didn't know it, I certainly wasn't going to make it any easier for him to discover. When I didn't respond, Soola shrugged.

"When we're done with that poultice, I have a special salve here. It will help the healing go much faster. If you do exactly as I say, it will be completely healed in three or four days. It's up to you."

I remained silent. There was nothing I wanted to say to Soola. And she let the silence between us grow until it felt like something alive, a palpable wall between us.

"Time," she finally said, holding out a hand into which, after another moment, I placed the poultice. "You'll have to let me apply the salve. It must be done properly, and you can't do it yourself."

I could if I had a mirror, I thought, then realized that a mirror was the very last thing in the world I wanted to see. Other than Rennirt himself. Our eyes met, and in that instant, I knew that she understood. I nodded slowly.

She turned around to get the candle so that she could see better. She handed it to me to hold while she extracted a pot from the basket. When she turned back to face me, I saw what I hadn't before in the dim light: her entire face was scored with raised, black lines. I stared as she dabbed the salve onto my cuts with a touch so gentle I scarcely felt it. The lines on her face chased each other in interlocking swirls, a design so complex it could take years to unlock its secrets. Had Rennirt done this to her, or was it simply a custom of her people?

Involuntarily, my hand started to reach up toward her face. When she noticed, she caught my eye. I froze, but she nodded permission.

The lines really were raised; it wasn't a trick of the candle-light. I stroked her cheek, wondering if the ridged scars felt my touch at all. She turned her head into my caress, and her eyes fluttered closed. A soft sigh escaped her lips.

When I let my hand drop back to my lap, she opened her eyes and said, "Yours won't be like mine. Master Ganwin used a different technique. Once it's healed, your skin will feel perfectly normal. The design will simply look like liquid silver. It will be especially beautiful in the moonlight."

Beautiful? *Beautiful?* How could lines carved into my face be beautiful? I wanted to scream, but the tenderness of what had just transpired stopped me. I simply sat there and watched Soola pack up her things to go. She pounded on the door with her fist, though I doubted anyone could hear. To my surprise, the door opened moments later.

"I'll be back in six hours for the next treatment," she said, then she passed through the door, taking the light and any last shreds of my happiness with her.

✦

To Lord Lorac~

It is my unfortunate duty to inform you that your son, Rennirt, is no longer welcome to study at the House of Willow. We have been lenient of his transgressions, not for your sake alone but for his as well. His power is mighty and he has great potential for good, if only he would discipline himself to his studies. We hoped that he would.

Alas, he has chosen to continue his dissolute and drunken behavior, going far beyond what is acceptable for a student and leaving us no choice but to permanently remove him from his course of studies and send him home to you.

Should you require further information, do not hesitate to call on us at Willow House.

~As ever at your disposal,
Pallan, Chief Sage, Order of the Willow

Twelve

Over the next few days—I supposed they were days, for I had no way to know—it was the regular visits from Soola and the occasional meals shoved through the slot near the bottom of the door that made me sure I was not dead. Down in that dungeon, it was dark—dark and silent and lonely. I began to understand what it must be like to be both blind and deaf. Sometimes I tried to sing or at least hum, but the sound fell flat, as if none but a fool could stay alive down here for long.

I lay for long hours, lost in my maejic. It could not free me physically, but I found my mind could ride it deep into my memories to relive the times of my life.

The first time it happened was when I first tried to meditate. I cleared my thoughts—an easy thing in this black, soundless hole. I sought my calm center. Hard to do when it roiled, caged deeply in my soul. I tried to open my inner senses and was glad to find that I could. I wanted to be free, I begged to be free.

And whereas my maejic usually took my spirit outside myself, now it took me inward.

I found myself deep in a memory, so deep it was almost real. I was a tiny thing, still a toddler. It was evening, barely dusk with the feel of Autumn on the air. A few candles burned in wall sconces in the main room of our cottage, but the roaring fire on the hearth provided most of the light. Breyard couldn't have been more than five, and he pranced naked around the room, battling some imaginary foe and making Mama and Papa laugh. I was warm and comfortable—and wet: I sat in a tin bath before the fire while Mama bathed me.

With sleeves rolled up past her elbows and her hair pulled back from her face, she looked young, not all that much older than I was now.

Papa sat in a wooden chair nearby. His hands were busy carving something, though from my vantage point near the floor, I couldn't tell what.

Breyard stabbed the air in front of him with an imaginary sword.

"Ooof!" exclaimed Papa. "I think you got him that time."

Breyard danced a little jig in glee. My chubby hands beat the top of the water, splashing it in all directions. Mama let out a small grunt.

"There, there, little one. Calm down, now. Tegar," she said, looking up at Papa, "the water is cooling."

Papa set down the things in his hands and crouched next to the tin bath, facing Mama. I looked from one to the other, Mama with droplets of water on her cheeks, Papa with his smooth, clean-shaven face and bits of grey beginning to show in his dark brown hair. They smiled at each other in an intimate way I couldn't have grasped then but understood now.

Papa placed a hand on each side of the bath, as if he were going to pick it up. But he didn't. He just stayed where he was, watching Mama finish bathing me in water that had begun to steam just a little. Every once in awhile, he gurgled at me to make me laugh.

When I came to myself in my dungeon, deep in the bowels of the earth, dark and silent, I wept.

+ + +

Another time when my maejic took me back into the past, the memory was of an evening when I was about nine years old. I'd been sick during the day—I could taste the sour flavor of illness even now—and had awakened in a sweat that had soaked my bedclothes. I felt better, for the day's fever had broken, but I was thirsty.

I threw back the damp covers and got out of bed. The cool stone of the cottage floor felt good on the soles of my sweaty feet. I padded to the pantry to get a drink. The cool water, dipped fresh from the cistern, slid down my parched throat.

Passing through the main room, I heard my parents' voices float in from the yard through the open window. They liked to go outside on a warm night, once Breyard and I were tucked into bed, and chat under the open sky. I'd asked Papa about that once, and he'd said they liked to watch the stars dance to the moon's music. When I asked if I could stay up to watch and listen, he'd kissed my forehead and said, "No, my sweet, you can't. You won't be able to see or hear it until you fall in love."

But this night, my parents seemed to be having one of their rare disagreements. I stopped, unable to keep myself from listening.

"I still don't like it," Mama was saying.

"I don't like it, either," Papa replied. "But it's for the best.

We simply can't risk anyone, not even they themselves, finding out the truth."

"How will sending them away keep them safe? How can anyone in the world protect them better than you can?"

Papa's sigh was so heavy I could almost feel its weight. "No one here can train them properly. At the academy, their thoughts will be filled with learning magic."

Learning magic! My heart leapt. I knew they must be talking about Breyard and me. I didn't stay to listen to any more, but dashed to my room, full of this secret. I got a fresh blanket from the chest next to my wardrobe and went back to bed. Just wait until I told Breyard in the morning!

But, of course, I'd forgotten the whole thing until now.

+ + +

During the long, black, silent hours, I had to fight off hallucinations. Sometimes I rubbed my knuckles against the rough stone wall, trying to use pain to keep myself sane. How long would I be kept down here? How long would my maejic be able to stave off madness?

Each session with Soola grew in importance until it seemed she was the be-all and end-all of my life. Each six-hour interval between her visits stretched into eternity.

+ + +

The last trip into my memories went to the Spring before I started at Roylinn Academy. Breyard, of course, was already studying there, so it was just Mama, Papa, and me.

Although it was past the time for Winter storms, a terrible

blizzard had struck the day before. The snow was so deep we couldn't see out the windows. Papa had spent much of the afternoon digging a path clear between the cottage and the outbuildings. We all slept in the front room that night, wrapped in blankets and covered in furs, the fire blazing to keep the room warm.

I'd awakened to find Papa putting on his heavy work boots. Mama lay next to me, still asleep.

"Where are you going?" I asked Papa in a whisper.

"To the lambing shed. Now go back to sleep."

"Why are you going there? It's the middle of the night."

"Shh. You'll wake your mother. I'm going because I'm needed."

"How do you know?" I asked, confused.

"I just do. Now, please, my sweet, just go back to sleep."

And now I sat up sharply, crying out in surprise. Papa was maejic, too! He must be!

My heart raced at the thought. It had always been a wonder to the people of our village that Breyard and I had such strong magic, since neither of our parents did. Now I understood the truth: Papa *did* have magic, and not just magic, but maejic, too.

Why then had he been so fearful about my maejic? Once he'd beaten me unmercifully at the mere suggestion, insisting that I never mention it again. When I'd recently discovered that I was maejic and that it was a capital offense, his reaction had made more sense.

Now there were so many things I wanted to ask him, but he was far from here, in a whole different world to which I might never return.

+ + +

When Soola next came, she held her candle near my face. With a half-smile, she felt my cheek with her free hand. I almost flinched from her touch before realizing that it didn't hurt. No burning, no stinging, no itching. As if it were back to normal.

"It's healed," Soola said in a soft, almost bemused voice. "You did well not to fiddle with it, to let the medicines do their work." Her eyes moved from their examination of my cheek to my own eyes. "It *is* beautiful. No matter what you fear."

I sucked in my breath in a tiny gasp. There were so many things I feared, but until now, I'd refused to use the word lest it bind me. Now that she'd said it, a torrent was loosed in me, freezing me in place and leaving me unable to speak as she stood up, pounded on the door, and left me. The door scraped shut with an air of finality.

Now that my fears were loosed, they chased each other within my soul. Would I be left here to die? Or simply to go mad? What had happened to Traz? Had Rennirt carved a mark onto his face, too? Where was Shandry? I didn't remember seeing her in the hut before Rennirt took away my sight. How was Grey coping with Xyla's illness? Would Xyla get well? Would any of us ever return to Hedra? And through it all, the worst fear of all: would I ever see Mama and Papa again?

+ + +

The sound of the door opening jerked me out of my thoughts. Light flooded into my cell, and I closed my eyes and turned my head away.

"Be getting up now," said a rough voice, but I cowered back into my corner. I put a hand over my eyes and tried to look out through the cracks between my fingers, but even that hurt. Then a large shadow interposed itself between me and the light. Rough hands gripped my upper arms and pulled me to my feet. "Don't be giving me any trouble, lassie, or I swear I'll rip out your tongue."

There was no question in my mind whether he was jesting. Eyes still closed, I stumbled out of the cell. The man gave me a push to the left, and I started walking. Before long, I was pushed to the right. A few steps later, I cracked my toes painfully. My eyes opened a slit. The stairs. Squinting against what only a few days ago I considered dim torchlight, I began to climb.

The guard behind me didn't force me to go any faster than I could, but he didn't let me stop, either. Up and up we went. By the time we reached the top, my eyes had mostly adjusted to the light, as long as I kept them shaded with a hand. My thighs burned from the effort as I tried to catch my breath.

The guard shoved me aside to unlock and open the door. I shivered where I stood, more with fear than with cold. He beckoned me through. Another guard stood watch on the other side, and when the first one pointed at the door, the second one made that grunting noise I'd heard before and locked it. Remembering what I'd just been threatened with, I suddenly understood what I hadn't even thought of before.

A woman in a military uniform stood leaning against the wall, arms crossed over her chest. She wrinkled her nose and scowled at me.

"Good thing I have orders to clean you up first." She strode off at a pace I could scarcely keep up with.

We went down the corridor, turned left, went a little farther and turned right. Through a doorway, then several more turns until it would've been impossible for me to retrace my steps. If I'd wanted to.

Finally she opened a door and led me into a room.

"Be fast about it," she said, pointing to a recessed area. "And put this on when you're done." The thing she tossed at me fell at my feet when I failed to react fast enough to catch it.

I picked up what turned out to be a shift of fine linen. The guard waved a hand impatiently toward the cubicle, and I went into it.

Where I found, luxury of luxuries, a small pool filled with steaming water. I didn't even care how such a thing could be. I peeled off my filthy clothes, only now noticing how bad they smelled.

"Toss me those rags," the guard said.

I did, and then I stepped into the water. It stung at first, but I didn't care. Ah, but to be clean again. I found a pot of soft soap on the far side, as well as a firm sponge. I scrubbed and scrubbed, then scrubbed some more at my skin, trying to remove not only the layers of dirt and filth and stink, but also the remembrance of the past days.

When I got out, my skin was red from the vigorous scouring, but at least I felt clean. I dried off with a towel I found on a shelf, then slipped on the shift. The guard told me to follow her, and with a sigh, I did.

I couldn't guess where she was taking me now, though I had a vague hope that it would involve food. What I didn't expect was for her to open a pair of ornately decorated doors, bow as she entered, then step aside, leaving me face-to-face with Rennirt.

✦

There is music in the starlight. Did you not know? Have you not heard? It has a beat of compelling sweetness, guiding one's steps into a delicate pattern. There it is now. Can you hear? A melody that whispers, a harmony that soothes. Together, they delight one's soul, giving power the taste of honey and the scent of rain-washed air. Ah, it tugs at my soul and calls me to join in the dance of the stars.

That twinkling sound—do you hear? Can you guess what it is? 'Tis the music of the stones. Ah, you expected a music deep and strong, did you? Nay. For it must be a light sound to be carried on the swirling currents of the stones. Take this. Cradle it in the palm of your hand. Join in the song and hold not back.

Every tree has its own voice. Some are buoyant and frothy, full of lightness and air. Some are ponderous and slow, singing of the deep truths of the world. Some flit between melody and harmony, joyous in their rhythm as they declare the glory of the earth like the night breeze plays across the sands.

Heavy beats the rhythm of the sun. Can you feel it luring your feet to follow its lead? An irresistible bass melody cannot help but draw you in. Feel its power in your soul. Feel its harmony in your heart. Take flight, my child. The bold pattern of the sunlight becomes evident in the dance. Let your spirit drink in the joy and refresh you.

Breathe in the rhythm; exhale the beat. Ride on the melody like the breeze. The air imbues all life with its music. Indeed, it is the first earth music most hear. Without air, there is no life. So, too, music. Pick up the harmony and float on it. Let it carry you away to a place of power, where your soul can be refreshed.

~from the teachings of Gedden, lore master

Thirteen

✦

I froze just outside the door. Rennirt rose to his feet, a smile of delight on his face. With difficulty, I suppressed the urge to run.

"We meet again at last," Rennirt said, as if we were old friends long parted. He took one of my hands, which I managed not to snatch away, and led me into the room.

It was an intimate sitting room, furnished with padded chairs and a settee upholstered with delicate needlework. There were dainty, spindle-legged tables, and a merry fire crackled in a fireplace. Candle sconces and framed paintings ornamented the walls. It was beautiful, and I hated it.

Rennirt led me to the center of the room and stopped me under the bright light of a crystal chandelier. Turning to face me, he placed a hand on each of my shoulders and examined the hateful mark on my cheek.

"Yes," he murmured. "Ganwin outdid himself this time. I will have to reward him with extra gold pieces." He lifted one hand and, with the lightest touch of a fingernail, traced a pattern. Though his touch was gentle, it left behind a trail of heat. "Not quite tattoo, not quite scarification. Beautiful. Now that I've mastered silver, I shall turn my attention to gold." At my startled frown, he chuckled. "Oh, yes, my dear. There is real silver in that pigment. Gives it its glitter, its shine. Now, come sit, and we shall chat."

I took the seat he indicated, but I didn't relax, didn't let down my guard.

He sat in a chair facing me, and it was all too reminiscent of the last time we'd been seated in such an arrangement. A chill crept down my spine, and I tried not to shiver in response.

Rennirt put his elbows on the arms of his chair and pressed his long, slender fingers together under his chin. His emerald eyes bored into mine, and though I wanted to look away, I found I couldn't. What exactly did he want of me?

And then I felt something riffling my thoughts, as if thumbing through the pages of the book of my mind. Almost instinctively, I began to block, a maejic technique used to keep external vibrations from one's spirit so as not to be overwhelmed; it was the only defense I could think of now.

Rennirt blinked. And frowned. He pursed his lips, and I could feel the thread of his thought trying to break through. I held my breath and concentrated. Whatever Rennirt wanted from me, I wasn't going to let him have it.

The battle went on, for moments maybe, or maybe hours. It ended when Rennirt leaned back in his chair, eyes closed as if in exhaustion. He raised a hand and pointed at me.

"You *will* give me what I want." The left side of my face began to grow warm. "Sooner or later."

He stood up, and my face burned hotter. I put a hand to it, but the skin felt normal to my touch, cool even. Yet from within, it felt as if it were on fire. Rennirt walked out of the room, slamming the door behind him. My face grew hotter and hotter, as if the skin must burst into flame soon.

In agony, I looked around the room for something to cool the fire. But there was nothing. No, wait. There must be a window behind the curtains and, being exposed to the cooler air outside, it might help. I stumbled over and pulled the heavy fabric aside. A black void of glass. I pressed the side of my face against it, hoping for relief.

But the fire burned hotter.

I fell to the ground, sobbing in terror. What kind of power could do this? How could I counteract it? I tried to withdraw my mind into myself, but the pain was too great to ignore.

I lay there shivering in the chill air and frequently crying aloud in pain, while my face smoldered. As time passed, the heat began to fade, little by little. When I felt I could move again, I sat up and leaned against the nearest window. The cold went straight through the fabric of my shift and into my spine. Hoping the magic was wearing off, I once again pressed my cheek to the glass.

The fire re-ignited.

The shock of it made me scream.

Deep within my soul, I heard laughter.

I lay on the floor without moving for a long time. The burning slowly dissipated, like coals burning themselves out, and still I lay there.

I considered my situation. Rennirt wanted something from me: my power. I must resist him, that much was clear. But how, when he was so strong and had such an effective tool to control me.

The solution seemed elegantly simple when I finally thought of it. And what I must do first was get myself under control. Somewhat shakily, I rose to my feet. I felt weak, as if I'd not eaten in ages. Then I realized that, in truth, I hadn't. No help for that now. I padded around the room, hoping that the beautiful elements of it would soothe my spirit.

The paintings that hung in their carved wooden frames were exactly what one would expect to find in any aristocratic home: portraits, hunting scenes, still lifes, and scenery. All very beautiful, yet filled with details that made them foreign. Hounds of unusual breeds I didn't recognize, unfamiliar fruits in amongst the ones I knew, and a flat, barren land with little foliage and much sky. The people were mostly a dark-skinned, handsome folk who dressed in brighter colors people wore back home.

And then a thought struck me. Maybe people from this part of Hedra also had dark skin. I'd never had occasion to meet anyone from Ultria, for there had been little trade between it and Alloway in my lifetime.

Well, be that as it may, it had nothing to do with my own here-and-now. I went to the settee and sat down. I wanted to rest only for a moment, but without realizing I'd done it, I curled into a ball and fell asleep.

At first, red dragons filled my dream. Xyla was there, so these must be her babies. Yet they were grown. They flew through the air in sweeping patterns, their paths crossing and curling into intricate knots. Then everything went fuzzy and out of focus. My blood boiled and my flesh roasted. A laughing hand gave me a skinful of water to drink, but took it away before I was satisfied. If only the heat would break. Ah, but for a cool stream in which to dip my toes.

A rattling sound jarred me out of my sleep. A girl about my own age walked in carrying a tray. I sat up, trying to shake off the dream. It had felt so real, as if my whole body were actually on fire. The girl set the tray on the table, and I saw that it held a basket of steaming bread whose fresh-baked scent began to fill the room and make my stomach rumble. There was also soft cheese and leten. She lifted a cover to reveal a bowl of soup. And best of all, there was a large pitcher of water—enough, maybe, to quench my thirst at last.

When I'd finished eating, the girl reappeared. She went to the curtains and opened them wide, letting in a flood of sunlight. Sunlight! It must have been years since I last saw it.

Next thing I knew, I stood at the window gazing out. On the other side was a courtyard, around the corners of which lay wide flowerbeds, mostly dormant now but with buds beginning to swell with the stirrings of Spring. A stone fountain rose from a pool in the center. The pool was surrounded by a lawn on which the morning dew sparkled. Boxwood hedging, less than a foot high, was laid out in a complex design: a labyrinth or, perhaps, a knot. I touched my cheek with trembling fingers but felt nothing there, not even the fine lines of scar tissue.

What did it look like? I took a deep breath, steeled myself, and focused my eyes on the glass in front of me. But though I could see a vague reflection of my face, I couldn't see any detail, certainly not any thin silver lines.

I felt more than heard Rennirt enter the room. My shoulders

stiffened, and I forced myself to relax. I couldn't let my body give away my plan.

He cleared his throat and I turned around, composing my face into a suitably subdued expression.

"Let us see if you have now learned your lesson. Please, sit." He gestured to the chair I'd sat in the day before. With purposely halting steps, I walked across the room and took my seat, keeping my eyes downcast.

Rennirt sat across from me. I stared at my hands in my lap, bracing my mind for the assault I knew would come any moment.

Yet, like a cat with a mouse, he toyed with me.

It was unsettling, sitting there in the silent room, waiting for an attack that didn't come. Then, like the gossamer wings of a dragonfly, I felt the touch of his thought in my mind. I resisted, as I knew he expected me to. He made an inarticulate sound, and I put more effort into my resistance. Once begun, the pressure grew unabated. I closed my eyes, putting as much of my power into blocking him as I could.

The tension in my entire body increased, and my muscles knotted up. My shoulders hunched until they seemed to be at my ears.

Just when the pressure became unbearable, I relaxed, body, soul, and mind. Collapsing backward in my chair, I could now only hope my plan would work—that, thinking I'd completely given in, Rennirt would range freely and not notice that I continued to block him from my maejic.

It was a risky strategy, but it was my only hope. To continue actually resisting him would only encourage him to work harder to break down my barriers and search more thoroughly.

Rennirt let out an audible sigh, as if he, too, were relieved. I kept my eyes closed and formed a black sphere in my mind and focused all my thought on that.

"A red dragon," he muttered, the words startling me. "A handy steed to have at beck-and-call."

I concentrated on breathing and on the black sphere.

"But whence?" he whispered, so softly I barely heard it. "Whence comes your power?"

A breath in. Black sphere. Breath out.

A distant sound of commotion began to grow. I tried to block it out, to keep concentrating on the void in my mind, but soon it was right outside the room.

The door opened with a crash that made me jump. Rennirt was on his feet before I could turn around to see this new threat.

"You will release her *now*," a loud voice boomed across the room.

I twisted around to see a tall man, taller and darker than even Rennirt, standing just inside the doorway, his rich red cloak billowing around him from the force of his movements. Or maybe from the force of the power that emanated from him and filled the room. He took another step, and two more people came in behind him: a man and a woman, also dressed in red cloaks.

"You have far overstepped your bounds this time," said the first man, and I noticed that the words almost formed a melody, as if he were singing. "The time has come to put you in your place. And to make sure you stay there."

The man's eyes, which were a brown so deep they almost looked black, fell on me. A thrill went through me, but one of joy, not fear. I couldn't seem to move, though. My mind hadn't truly unfrozen yet, and my thoughts were disheveled. He smiled, not a threatening smile like Rennirt's, but one of gladness. My heart leapt, though for what reason I couldn't tell.

"Take her," the man said to the other. "Kelben and Breyard await." And now I jumped to my feet to go to these people.

"No!" shouted Rennirt behind me. "I do not recognize your authority here."

And I froze in place. Not of my own volition; no, something held me in place like an invisible net.

"You soon will have no authority, Rennirt, here or anywhere." The man thrust his hand toward me, palm out. The other two came nearer. I willed myself to break free of Rennirt's power. All I had to do was put one foot in front of the other. Concentrating hard, I made a foot move. Not a full step, but at least something.

Then the man and the woman reached me. One on each side, they picked me up and carried me out of the room.

"No! I will not allow . . . " Rennirt's words were cut off.

When we reached the front door, the man set me on my feet. The two of them took my hands and we dashed out and down the stairs.

There on the wide lawn before the door, stood a huge red dragon. For a moment, I thought it was Xyla, until I realized that this one was even bigger than she.

"It is good to see you at last," said a deep, musical voice inside my head. "I am Kelben.

"I'm honored," I replied, almost automatically because there were too many things happening too quickly, and I felt overwhelmed. I now saw that there were two more red dragons standing on the lawn, and several more circling overhead. Red-robed figures moved toward me, and, best of all, Breyard rode astride Kelben.

I am surrounded by a kaleidoscope of wood. It encircles me all around, above and below even. Power envelopes me, holding me tight.

I have always loved wood, but the trees from which these branches grew are bitter. I try to escape, but there is no way out. Every direction I turn, I find a maze that dazzles my senses.

I thirst. I burn. I cry out for water, for even just a moment's release.

And Anazian laughs.

Fourteen

B reyard grinned and waved at me, and I ran to Kelben;
indeed, I doubt any magic would've been strong enough
to stop me.

"Mount up, little one," Kelben said. "I shall soon fly you
far away."

I scrambled up, needing a hand from Breyard, and was
soon seated far above the ground, my brother behind me
holding me in a tight hug. I leaned back against him and felt
a little of my tension slip away.

"How can this be?" I asked. "Who are these people? And
how can you possibly be here?"

Breyard shook his head. "Too much to tell now. I'll fill
you in later, once we're all safe."

There was a muffled sound of a distant explosion. I
looked back and saw for the first time the place in which I'd
been imprisoned.

A castle stood basking in the Spring sunshine, its yellow
stones almost gleaming. It might have been pretty to someone like me who wasn't accustomed to such things, had it not
exuded such an air of threat. The evil was palpable, though
perhaps it was only my imagination.

I had only moments to take this all in before everything
seemed to happen at once. The man who'd stayed behind

sped out the front door, his red robe flowing behind him. He ran straight to Kelben, making a leap that must be propelled by magic and landing softly in front of me. The other two mounted the dragons standing nearby as figures began to pour out the front entrance of the castle.

With a rush of wings and wind that blew my hair away from my face, all three dragons were airborne. Looking down, I saw that the buildings were laid out in a labyrinth design that quickly grew indistinct as we flew away.

It was cold aloft, and I wished I had heavier clothes. I shivered, and Breyard held me tighter.

"She's freezing!" he shouted.

The man in front of me looked back, a frown of concern furrowing his brow. He nodded once, and a moment later the dragon swept around into a new direction.

Below us, the forest began to thin and break up. Ahead, the land flattened out and took on a yellowish color.

Kelben's voice spoke in my head. "We will go to Delaron. Your young friend Traz is there."

"Traz! I don't understand. How can he be in Delaron?" That didn't make any sense. I began to think I really must be dreaming after all. I shivered again, and Breyard rubbed his hands on my thighs in a vain effort to warm my legs.

"I will let Traz tell you his story," said the dragon.

The flat, yellow land below us sped by. Here and there were patches of dark green or brown. The air had grown dry, making me thirsty again.

Before long, a cluster of buildings alongside a good-sized

lake appeared ahead of us. Breyard pointed and said, "That's Delaron."

"How can Traz be there?" I asked, but the dryness in my throat made it come out as little more than a whisper, and the wind stole the words away.

My head felt muddled, as if it were stuffed full of cotton. Traz in Delaron? Breyard here? I couldn't make sense of it, no matter how hard I tried.

Then we were heading downward toward the sprawling city built next to the lake. Breyard's arms tightened around me as I leaned back against the angle of descent.

Before we landed, I caught a close-up glimpse of the deep blue water surrounded by strange trees that looked like little more than trunks with a bit of fluffy foliage on top.

Then we were on the ground, and the man leapt off the huge dragon's back and landed lightly on the ground. Breyard helped me dismount in the more conventional way. The soft, silky sand cushioned my landing but burned the soles of my feet. I let out a yelp of pain. Breyard thudded down next to me and lifted me into his arms.

Someone shouted my name, and I thought I recognized Traz's voice. I swiveled my head around to see, but as if that movement took up my final reserves, my equilibrium failed. For a brief moment, everything swirled around me, and then I passed out.

+ + +

My eyes fluttered open. At first, I feared I was back in my cell, but there was too much light. Then I thought I must be in Rennirt's sitting room, until my brother's face floated into view, his hazel eyes dark with concern.

"Breyard?" I asked in a whisper. "Is it really you? It wasn't a dream?"

He smiled in relief. I heard a sound of dripping water, and next thing I knew he was placing a cool, damp cloth on my forehead. "No, it wasn't a dream at all. How are you feeling?"

"A little woozy and confused. And hot."

"Typical. She complains of being hot in the coolest place around." Traz's voice from nearby startled me into trying to sit up, but dizziness forced me to lie back again.

"Careful," Breyard said. "Halla said you need to take it easy 'til your system gets over the shock. Lie still while I get you something to drink."

I started to reach for his hand, not wanting him to leave my side—not yet, anyway—but he was too fast and I was too sluggish. Then Traz was there, giving me one of his grins. I lifted my hand to touch his face.

"It's really you," I said, smiling when he blushed. "But how?"

He looked around, then leaned down close to me. "I'll tell you the whole story later, when you're feeling better, but the gist of it is this. Shandry had gone outside the hut to check on Dyster. She heard those people coming, so she hid from them. That evil guy, that was Rennirt, you know."

I nodded. "Believe me, I know."

"Well, Shandry rescued me in the morning after they took you away, and we made double-time here. As soon as Botellin heard what happened to you, he and a few others blasted out of here like lightning. Shandry took some others to Xyla. And—"

But he cut himself off and sat straight up, a look of innocence on his face that would've made anyone who knew him well suspicious. A moment later, Breyard came to the other side of my bed with a mug. He slid an arm under my shoulders and lifted me gently, just enough so I could drink the clear, cold water.

"Sip it slowly," he said. "Halla said that gulping it down will give you a stomachache."

I thought a stomachache would be a small cost to relieve my thirst, but Breyard let me have only tiny drinks. I resolved to get him back one day.

A tiny woman with short, curly hair and green eyes walked up and put a wrinkled hand on Breyard's shoulder.

"I'll take over now, lad. If you don't mind."

He stepped back, letting her take his place near my shoulder, then hovered next to her as if not wanting to let me out of his sight. For a change, I didn't resent his protectiveness; indeed, I actually appreciated it. Not that I'd ever admit it to him, though.

"I'm Halla, my dear," the old woman said, picking up my hand as gently as if I were made of fine crystal and taking my pulse. "These two have told me your name is Donavah." Her voice was soothing and her eyes jolly, but her words carried the weight of a master. She must be the healer.

"Yes, ma'am," I said, licking my lips as my voice came out as a croak.

"You may have more to drink in a few minutes." She set

my hand down, patted it, and felt first my right cheek and then my left, frowning but saying nothing about the mark there. "You have had a bit of a shock, and I want you to stay here a few more days to regain your strength. I trust you will have two attentive caregivers." She smiled at Traz and Breyard. "You may talk here quietly until she sleeps again."

Breyard and Traz nodded in agreement, and Halla left, saying something about a light but nutritious meal.

Breyard helped me to drink some more water, and this time when he lifted me, I didn't get dizzy, so I asked him to help me sit up properly.

That felt much better. The cloth Breyard had put on my forehead only a few minutes before slipped to my lap, and when I picked it up, I found it was practically dry.

Traz took it and set it next to a large bowl on the bedside table. Breyard sat on a chair, just looking at me without saying a word. For a moment, I stared back. Finally, I couldn't stand it any longer.

"What are you doing here?"

"Well, that's an interesting story," he said, then didn't say any more. His eyes took on an unfocused look.

"Maybe you could tell me sometime today? Before I burst from wondering about it?"

He focused back on me. "Oh, sorry. Got distracted for a moment there."

I looked at the wall behind me, but that's all it was, a plain wall without even any pictures on it. The windows were on the other side of the room, though from where I was, the only thing I could see out of them was the bright blue sky.

Breyard continued. "You know about the fight in the dragon pit. Traz told me all about the part you and he played in it." I nodded. "Well, all I knew at the time was that a dragon was going to kill me. Just before they shoved me out there, they shaved my head, stripped off my clothes, and doused me with some foul-smelling liquid they called 'dragon bait.'

"I'd been in the dark so long that when I entered the pit, the sun blinded me. But I could hear the noise of the crowd rising up all around me. And then, when my sight cleared, all I could see was this huge red dragon."

He stopped speaking, and his eyes tightened as if the memory of that day still brought him pain.

"Xyla," I said softly, trying to bring his attention back to his story.

"Yes, Xyla. When she grabbed me up in her mouth, I figured it was all over, but she didn't hurt me at all. Everything went sparkly, and hot and cold, and my ears were filled with strange noises like musical explosions. But that sounds stupid. Maybe it was all a dream. I can't remember it very clearly. Xyla landed, had me mount her properly—"

Traz's giggle interrupted Breyard. "Bet that was comfy, you being naked and all."

"Traz!" I exclaimed as Breyard blushed.

"Well, it's true," Traz said, not even trying to hide his mirth.

"But you don't have to say it."

"It's all right," Breyard said. "He's right, anyway. That whole journey was something I'd rather forget, but it was better than the alternative. And Xyla brought me here, to Delaron."

A million questions rushed into my head, leaving me unable

to articulate any of them. Why hadn't Xyla simply returned right away with Breyard? Why wait here so long? Now I remembered him saying that he'd stayed here more than a year. Why? Then another clear thought rang through all the questions.

"There are two of Xyla here!" I exclaimed.

Breyard shook his head. "No, three."

He was right, of course. She'd come here to Stychs as a baby to grow. Then she'd brought Breyard. And now Traz, Grey, and me. The idea of it took my breath away and made my head hurt.

"Are the other two here? In Dealron, I mean?"

"No. The younger one is with the rest of the youngsters at a place called Rinkam."

"A dragon nursery?" The image that thought conjured made me smile.

Breyard smiled, too. "Yes, I suppose you could say that. The other one, the one I'm here with, well, as soon as Traz explained the situation, Botellin sent her away. She and a few other dragons went to Altan. She said she'll come back once everything is resolved."

It was a moment before the significance of what Breyard said sank in. "She said? You can speak to her?"

He bit his lower lip and gave me a sidelong look.

"You're maejic, too!" I exclaimed.

He nodded slowly. "I discovered it when I was in Erno's prison. One of the dragonmasters denounced me. It didn't, shall we say, improve my plight."

Halla came back just then carrying a tray with food on it.

She shooed the boys away, promising they could come back after I'd eaten and rested a bit.

There was a thick soup that was tasty without being too savory; a bowl of red, green, and pale yellow beans with melted butter; two pieces of flatbread; and a cup of hot herb tea. I didn't feel hungry until the aroma of the soup filled my nostrils. Halla watched with a satisfied look on her face as I began to eat.

She pointed to a small bell that hung from the wall next to the bed. "Just ring when you're done, and someone will come to take the tray. Then I want you to try to sleep again."

"But I've only just woken up. I'm not tired, and I'm feeling better every minute."

She smiled in the kindly aggravating way of healers everywhere. "You might not feel tired now, but you need to rest a bit more before I'll release you."

"But I have to get back to Xyla—"

She put a finger to her lips. "Just eat. Then sleep. We'll see after that." She left my bedside.

I looked around the infirmary as I ate. There were only three others, though there were sixteen beds, and we were spread around the room as if to give as much privacy as possible. Two of the others were men. The older one sat up studying a piece of parchment while the younger one had a tray on which he was playing some sort of solitaire card game. The third person lay sleeping, and I couldn't tell if it was a man or a woman.

When I finished eating, I rang the bell as Halla had instructed. It gave off a pleasant note that remained steady and didn't die away until a dark girl about my age came to my bed and pointed at it.

"I'm Jinna," she said with a cheery smile. "I'll be your attendant while you're here. Is there anything I can get for you before you sleep?"

"Well, actually..." I started, feeling the first signs that the tea had gone right through me.

"Oh! Yes, of course," Jinna said, immediately catching on. "I'll take you."

She helped me out of bed, producing a thin robe and slippers from under the bed. The facility was just a short walk away, but by the time I climbed back into my bed, I was worn out.

Jinna put the robe and slippers back where they came from, asked once again if I needed anything, then took the tray and left.

I lay for awhile, not sure whether I was tired enough to fall asleep. My mind was filled with too many thoughts to be able to catch hold of any of them. The journey to Delaron, everything that had happened with Rennirt, the rescue by the dragons, and now finding Breyard here. Trying to put all the pieces together made my head spin, and eventually I did drop off.

In my dream, I walked through a dark tunnel toward a dim light at the far end. When I came out, it was to step into a cave lit only by glowing embers. Something lay on the ground just ahead of me: a long, thin bundle wrapped in black cloth. I drew nearer.

The bundle moved, and I realized that it was me, sleeping. That brought me to a halt. Before I could puzzle out the meaning, a cloaked figure stepped from the shadows. It moved silently and smoothly, as if it were floating instead of walking.

It reached the sleeping me and crouched down, placing a hand on my head—a hand from which power flowed so thick I could see its tendrils encasing my whole upper body.

A voice floated on the air, and I strained to catch the words. "Your move." Why was that familiar? "Your move." The flavor of the words left behind a rancid aftertaste.

The crouching figure moved slightly, and I caught a glimpse of the person's face. A handsome face with strong features. Rennirt! My heart almost stopped. But no. This person was shorter than he and wider in the shoulders. And had much lighter skin.

Anazian!

Yes. Now I recognized his chiseled features and well-groomed hair.

"No!" I cried out. "Get away from me!"

He looked up from the sleeping me to the watching me, and his gaze went straight to my heart like lightning. He rose to his feet, pulling back his hood. His smile lacerated my soul.

"No!" I cried out again.

His lips parted.

"Donavah."

"No! Get away from me!" I wanted to flee but couldn't seem to move.

"Donavah! Wake up!"

✦

A half-played game of Talisman and Queen lies before me, the jewel pieces glowing as they sit on the black velvet, embroidered with glittering silver thread. The Queen's Heart, made of lapis lazuli, gleams at the center. Ranged about are the Talismans: mine, topaz; my opponent's, amethyst.

I cannot see against whom I play. Shrouded in shadow, the brooding presence stands, absorbing energy and my concentration. It seems to suck the very air from the room. I can scarce breathe.

The game is almost won. My heart tells me that with a single move, I will Secure the Queen's Heart. But my brain is frozen, unable to make sense of the game pieces. A wrong move, and my enemy will take all.

A voice breaks the silence—a familiar male voice that echoes around the room growing in power instead of fading away.

"Your move," it says.

A bright light shines, exploding the darkness.

"Perhaps you should give up and go home. Yes, that would be a plan. Home, where all is not as you left it," the voice says again, taking the last of the air with it.

I fall into a black pit of nothingness.

And then I awake.

Fifteen

I snapped out of my dream with a start that left me breathless. Breyard was leaning over me, hands on my shoulders, gently shaking me. I could hear my own ragged, shuddering breaths as I gulped the air.

Eyes dark with concern, Breyard asked, "Are you all right?"

I closed my eyes and reopened them just to make sure I'd really woken up.

"Yes," I said, my voice dry and harsh. "Bad dream."

Breyard, who I now saw was wearing strangely bright clothes made of some shiny fabric that gleamed even in the dimly lit infirmary room, let go and poured me a cup of water from the pitcher on the bedside table. "Here. Maybe this will help."

I sat up and took the cup. The water tasted sweet and cooled the fever of my dream.

"Want to tell me about it?" Breyard asked.

"It was so weird," I replied.

"Oh, and most dreams aren't?"

I shot him a look of surprise, only to find him grinning. He turned the chair so that he could sit facing me. "All right, I'll shut up and let you tell."

I took a deep breath and let it out in an audible sigh. "It was Anazian."

"Who or what is that?"

Right. Breyard wouldn't know about that. And I realized I couldn't tell him, because when he returned to Hedra, the whole thing would be part of his future. I'd have to keep the details vague.

"He's a mage. Back home. But the thing is that he said something to me that I'd been dreaming about before we came here." I told Breyard about the strange dreams of playing Talisman and Queen, and my opponent saying, "Your move."

"Do you think it means anything?" Breyard asked.

I shook my head slowly. "I don't know what it could mean."

He took my hand in both of his, which were warm and comforting. "Then forget it. It's probably nothing. I came by to check on you, see how you're doing." His eyes flicked to my left cheek, but he left *that* question unasked.

"I'm all right. I just want to get back to Xyla. And back home." A lump rose in my throat. Home. To Mama and Papa. Where I could be safe.

As if to stave off my impending tears, Breyard guffawed. "Home? And miss all this excitement?"

His strategy didn't work. My heart was still too raw. "Excitement?" It came out of me like a river bursting a dam. "Excitement? Being attacked by traitors and dragonmasters? Being chased into a whole other world? Being imprisoned and … and … " I yanked my hand out of his and covered my cheek " … having someone cut into your face? If that's the kind of excitement you're after, you can have it!" By this time, tears were streaming down my face.

Breyard looked stricken. "That's not … oh … " He moved to sit on the edge of the bed, and he gathered me into his arms.

I wept. And wept. All the bitterness of those long, dark hours came spewing out of me. Breyard simply held me, patting my back every once in awhile or whispering, "It'll be all right," in a soothing way.

Eventually the storm calmed. I still clung to my brother in a way I hadn't done for years, not since we were small. It felt good to be held in his strong arms, almost as good as it had felt to be held by Grey, although in a very different way.

Grey! What was he going to think when he saw me next? Had I not spent all my tears, the image of him turning away from me in disgust would've set me off again.

Exhausted, as one always is after an emotional release, I finally let go of Breyard and leaned back against my pillow. Using the end of his sleeve, he wiped first my right cheek and then my left. Was it my imagination, or did his hand falter as it touched the mark on my face? It might not burn anymore the way Rennirt had made it do, but it burned in my imagination all the same.

"Go back to sleep," Breyard said, his voice gentle and full of caring. "We'll talk more later."

I saw now that curtains had been drawn over the windows, most of the lamps were out, and the other three patients all lay sleeping—or, if my outburst had awakened them, perhaps pretending to sleep. I nodded.

"Want me to sit with you a bit longer?"

I almost shook my head, not wanting to appear needy. But the truth was that, for now at least, I did need him. "Yes, please," I whispered, then lay down. He pulled the light blanket up over me, stroked my hair, and sat back down.

Once or twice before I fell asleep, I opened my eyes a crack, and he sat there, still as a statue, an inscrutable look on his face.

If I dreamt the rest of the night, I didn't remember it when I awoke. At which time I found Traz, wearing bright yellow pajamas, sitting where Breyard had been.

The lamps no longer burned, and daylight set the still-closed curtains aglow. The other patients slept.

Traz broke into a grin when he saw me looking at him. "You're awake," he whispered.

"That's what usually happens when the sun rises," I said, then I yawned. "How long have you been here watching me?"

"Not long," he said, still speaking softly. "I snuck down because I want to tell you something privately. Breyard was here dozing, so I sent him off to sleep and said I'd look after you." He rolled his eyes. "As if you need any looking after."

I sat up cross-legged in bed facing Traz, and we spoke in whispers.

"I still don't understand why you're here. What happened at the way station? Last I knew, those guards had half-kicked you to death."

He shuddered. "Yeah. They tied me up like a trussed pig, then left me there to die. But Shandry, well, like I said before, she was on watch when it happened. She felt some sort of threat, you know, the way you sometimes do with the vibrations and all that. She went out to investigate, and when she saw Rennirt and the guards, she hid outside.

"When they left with you in the morning, she rescued me, and we lit out for here as fast as we could."

"So Shandry turns out to be the hero in the end," I said, trying not to let my voice sound as sour as I felt.

Traz just said, "Yeah, she really is. She led one group of dragons to Xyla, and Breyard insisted on going with Botellin—that tall man you rode Kelben with, and he's the leader here—to get you. The plan was to take you straight to Xyla, too, but it turned out that you were too sick, so they brought you back here."

"Sick? I'm not sick."

"Or whatever. I don't know all this healing stuff. How are you feeling today, anyway?"

"Better," I replied. "But curious about another thing now. Why did you stay here? Why didn't you go with Shandry and the others?" He adored Xyla, and I couldn't imagine what would keep him here when he could go to her.

His face lit up and he leaned closer to me. "That's what I've been trying to tell you. Remember about the sittack and everything?"

"The sittack? Oh, right. That legendary beast you caught."

"Yeah, well, it turns out that what Shandry said was right. I'm a sage! And I can danse."

It was true that he looked as if he were going to spring up from his seat and break into a jig of excitement. I couldn't help but grin at his infectious enthusiasm.

"You're a sage! That's brilliant news! How did you find out?"

Just then a boy a little older than Traz walked in. He smiled at the two of us but didn't say anything as he pulled back the curtains and opened the windows. Traz wriggled with impatience until the other boy left. The air quickly freshened with the morning breeze, and the occasional sound of a bird singing or people walking past floated in as we talked on.

"It was amazing. When Shandry and I got here to Delaron, we found everyone gathered as if they knew we were coming. Which I thought was pretty weird. But they *did* know we were coming."

"How could they? Could Shandry, I don't know, communicate with the dragons or something?"

Traz shook his head, his face very serious now. "My staff."

"Huh?"

"My staff. It turns out it's an artifact of the danse. A powerful one. And the sages didn't know who or what was coming, but they'd felt the power of it. They'd just gathered to discuss whether to have one of the dragons investigate when we arrived."

"I don't understand. What is this danse you keep talking about? And how could you find something from Stychs in the middle of nowhere on Hedra?"

"Well, the danse is a powerful form of magic here—like maejic is back home. But I haven't had time to learn much more than that yet. That's why I stayed here instead of going with Shandry. I want to study danse.

"And the staff, well, no one knows for sure how it got to Hedra from here. There's some old legend about a danse master and dragon who disappeared. The staff was his at the time. When the sages learned that we'd come from Hedra, they decided that that ancient master and dragon went there."

I nodded, trying to follow everything. "I guess that makes sense. They didn't take it away from you, did they?"

He chuckled as he reached down and picked it up. "No. I was afraid they might, too. Lini was pretty intense about the whole thing, examining it and testing it and all."

"Lini?" I prompted.

"Oh, the danse master here. She's taken me on as a student. I thought she wanted the staff for herself, but she explained that it always chooses its keeper."

I wished he'd slow down a bit and explain things so I could follow him. On the other hand, it was clear that he could hardly contain his enthusiasm. And knowing how badly he'd wanted to be maejic, I didn't want to dampen his happiness.

The others began to stir just then, and, as if on cue, Halla came in. She made a stern face at Traz, but her eyes twinkled. He returned a look of mock innocence that almost made me burst out laughing.

The healer attended the others first. Traz said he was glad to see me looking so much better and that he'd be back later, then disappeared out the door. When Halla got to me, I was back under the covers but sitting propped up against my pillow.

"Well," she said with a smile, "your color has returned and you've a spark back in your eye. I daresay the worst of your shock is over, and perhaps a walk outside later can be allowed."

"So I can go to Xyla now?" My heart leapt at the thought of seeing her again, then promptly plunged again when I realized that Grey would be there, too—along with Shandry.

Halla put a cool hand on my forehead. "Not quite yet," she said. "Soon. Perhaps another day or two."

"But—"

"I know you feel better now, but I want to make sure you have your strength back before you go traipsing off into the mountains. Is not an extra day here better than falling sick there?"

Her eyes held mine until I nodded. "Yes, ma'am," I said in a dull way that I hoped sounded more acquiescent than I felt.

She left the infirmary then. I chafed in frustration. Knowing Xyla needed help, how could I just stay here cooped up with nothing to do? Even talking to Breyard and Traz didn't keep my mind entirely off Xyla. What if she died? Would we ever get home again?

I loved Xyla. She was as dear to me as my best friend, as my own family. We'd been through so many things the past months, each helping the other. I couldn't imagine life without her any more than I could imagine life without my sight. Nor did I want to.

I picked at the threads in my blanket, noticing for the first time just how thin it was—scarcely more than a sheet. And I noticed, too, how warm it was in the room.

Several loud trumpeting sounds came in through the windows, and, curious, I got out of bed and went across to the window opposite.

The sky was a rich blue in which the sun rode clear of all but the wispiest high clouds. A rock garden stretched out before me, with different-colored patches of gravel used to create visual texture, rather than lawn and hedging as I was accustomed to. Spiky plants that looked completely alien to me were positioned here and there, soaking up the heat and sun, and giving only patchy shade.

Beyond the rock garden was a strip of white roadway on which several groups of people traveled. They wore brightly colored clothing that stood out in sharp contrast to the pale colors of the land all around.

Beyond the road was a stretch of brilliant, white sand, and beyond that, the lake I'd seen from the sky. And sporting in the blue water—the source of the trumpeting noises—were several red dragons, some diving deep and bursting out again while others just floated on the surface.

I watched, entranced, for several minutes, until footsteps behind me distracted my attention. Four young people came into the room bearing trays of food. One was Jinna, another was the lad who'd opened the windows, and the other two lads were complete strangers. The three boys slowed down, eyeing me, until Jinna told them to get their sorry selves moving, the patients were hungry.

I walked over to my bed, but sat in the chair next to it instead of getting back in, wishing I could be out in the warm sunshine instead of stuck in here with nothing to do.

Breakfast consisted of cold grain softened with milk and leten, a bowl of berries and cut-up fruit I didn't recognize, and chilled tea. Everything was strange and exotic, and it captured my interest for at least a little while. I made Jinna sit in the other chair by my bed and tell me the names of the different fruits and describe what they looked like in their natural state.

Once I finished eating, she sat gossiping about people I didn't even know. When she mentioned the name of one particular boy several times, bragging about how good he was at climbing the tall trees with no branches to get the fruit at the top, how good he was at fishing, how he was the best singer in Delaron, I began to get suspicious.

Being coy, I asked, "Is this Nolon your brother?"

As expected, Jinna spluttered her denial, and even though her skin was dark, she still blushed quite satisfactorily. I couldn't help laughing, too, and soon we were giggling about the different boys in our lives.

"Your brother isn't bad," she said.

"Oh, please. You sound just like Loreen, one of my friends back home. She moons over him constantly, and her eyes go all gooey at the mere mention of his name."

"But you have to admit he's handsome."

"I don't have to admit any such thing." The truth was that people always said we looked very much alike, except that he had hazel eyes while mine were dark brown. And while I didn't think of myself as especially pretty, I definitely didn't like to think of myself as *handsome*.

But that made me think of what my face must look like now. The smile fell from my lips and I raised my hand to my cheek. Jinna immediately picked up on my sudden change of mood and stopped laughing.

"What does it really look like?" I asked, not meeting her eyes.

She reached up and moved my hand away, then stroked that side of my face lightly. The touch of her hand sent shivers through me, and I closed my eyes. She stopped and simply held the palm of her hand against my cheek. I tried not to cry.

"I can't tell you what you want to hear," she said. "It won't ever go away."

Next thing I knew, she kissed both cheeks and then my forehead. "It doesn't make you any less a beautiful person."

The touch of her hands and of her lips went straight to my heart. Like a healing balm, they soothed the edges of my pain. I felt my spirit grow calm. When I opened my eyes, something inside me unclenched, and I burst into laughter.

✦

I hereby proclaim that the administration of Lake Delaron and its environs, as delineated on the map, reverse, be given over to the sage community, rent free, in perpetuity until such time as they choose to vacate it, at which point it shall revert to the Crown.

This is done with reference to the application made by Master Sage Larissa, and as a reward for longtime service to the Crown performed by the aforesaid community.

Thus have I decreed, thus shall it be, so say I.

~Morinda Queen Royal

Sixteen

Jinna joined my laughter. The other patients looked over at us, and the older one rolled his eyes and shook his head, which served only to make me laugh harder.

Once I got myself back under control and was wiping away the laugh-tears, Jinna took my breakfast things.

"Try to rest some more," she said, "and with luck, Halla will let you go for a walk later."

I just nodded. I didn't feel like resting any more. Perhaps the promise of a change of scenery might make the boredom easier to bear.

But it didn't. Just about the time I got up the courage to go ask the man playing cards to teach me his game, I sensed a disturbance out in the passageway.

A rush of power blew in through the open doorway like a gust of wind. It tickled my nose and made me feel like I was going to sneeze.

" …for a few more days." Halla's voice trickled in behind the wave of power.

"I appreciate your concern," replied a deep, musical voice. "But unless you have something concrete, I really must insist."

And with that, Botellin, the man who'd rescued me from Rennirt, strode into the room. He wore black trousers and boots and a shiny white sleeveless shirt that laced loosely up the front. His attire showed off his fit physique, and though he must be about the same age as my father, I couldn't imagine Papa wearing clothes such as these. But what was most noticeable was the magic that swirled around him. Traz had mentioned he was the leader of the community here, and I could well believe it.

He walked over to my bedside and smiled down at me from his great height. It felt awkward just sitting there in bed, and I wondered if I should stand up or something. Halla stood on the other side of the bed and placed a hand on my shoulder.

Then Botellin spoke to me, and his voice commanded all my attention, heart, mind, and soul.

"Welcome to Delaron, my child, though the words be spoken late. How do you feel?"

His words cradled me within their strength. Botellin sat down, his dark eyes intent on mine. I felt as if I were the only person in the whole world other than him, as if I were someone important, someone meaningful.

"I'm ... I'm fine," I stammered. "Much better than yesterday."

Botellin chuckled. "I daresay. I apologize for bungling your rescue."

"Bungling it? I don't ... I mean, thank you." There might be no threat from this man, but his power and intensity scrambled my thoughts, leaving me tongue-tied and scarcely able to put a coherent sentence together.

Halla's hand squeezed my shoulder. "You're frightening her, you lump of a man," she said in a gentle voice.

"No," I said quickly, not wanting him to get that idea.

Botellin closed his eyes. A moment later, the power swirling around us settled, calmed, then disappeared.

"Forgive me," he said. "I have come here anxious to meet you, forgetting to put on the demeanor appropriate to the sickroom." He looked up at Halla, eyebrows raised.

"Oh, you're as impossible as ever, and well you know it," she said, giving him a stern look that was belied by the smile in her eyes.

He grinned and leaned closer to me. "And still the woman complains."

Baffled, I couldn't think of anything to say.

Botellin turned his attention back to the healer. "You don't need to watch over our guest like a mother hen. I'm not going to eat her, interrogate her, or hurt her in any way." Halla didn't budge. "I *promise*."

Halla stood up slowly. "If he tires you, child, ring the bell. I will rescue you immediately."

When she'd gone, Botellin took my hand in his. I still didn't know what to say, so I remained quiet, though it felt both awkward and comforting to sit there with my hand being held by such a powerful man.

"Rescue," he finally said. "I must apologize that mine was so late."

"But you couldn't have known until—"

He waved my words away. "I keep a watch on Rennirt. He wields his power indiscriminately and with abandon, and I have made it my duty to try to prevent his most egregious abuses. But some slip past." He reached up and touched my left cheek. "I'm so, so sorry."

A lump rose in my throat at Botellin's tenderness, but I swallowed past it, determined not to cry.

"You are so brave, so strong," he continued. "I would like to get to know you better before you must return."

"Then you know? But, of course, you must." He would know about all of Xyla's visits here. Plus, Breyard had been here for a few months. By now, Botellin would've spoken to Traz and must know the bones of my story, too. "I really want to go to Xyla now. I need to be with her until she's better."

"Of course. As soon as Halla assures me you are strong enough, you shall go to her."

"I feel strong enough now."

He patted my hand. "I'm sure it will be soon, only a matter of a few days. But you see how the master healer rules her roost here, and not even I can gainsay her." His eyes twinkled. "Regain your strength as quickly as you can. We will talk more soon."

When he left the room, the air itself seemed to change, as if the power that surrounded him were a separate presence that went with him. The light no longer shone quite as brightly, and the edges of things didn't have quite as sharp a focus. I wondered what it would be like to have so much power yet be able to act as if you were completely unaware of it.

After lunch, Breyard came by again. He wore green leggings and a bright blue tunic belted with a red sash. He laughed when I put up a hand as if to protect my eyes.

"I know, I know," he said. "But you get used to the colors after awhile."

"I doubt it. But what's the fabric, anyway? I've never seen such strange stuff before."

"They call it *thillin*. It has the interesting property of keeping you cool during the heat of the day and warm when it cools off at night."

"But why does it have to be so bright?"

Breyard shrugged. "Why do we wear such dull clothes back home?"

"Maybe because the dyes are so expensive?"

"Piddling details. Anyway, Halla says you can go out for a bit, so I've come to take you for a walk. Delaron is a place such as you have never seen before!"

He bent down and pulled some things from under the bed. I wondered if there was a treasure chest down there or something. "Change into these. I'll wait for you here."

This time when I got out of bed, I looked and saw a shelf underneath on which were the robe and slippers from earlier and several more pieces of bed linen. I carried the clothes to the private cubicle that was generally used for other things. There was a knee-length purple skirt and a cream-colored tunic with a blue-green sash. I felt like a troubadour getting ready to go out on stage when I looked down at myself. Well, if everyone dressed like this, perhaps I wouldn't stand out.

Breyard had sandals for me, and when I'd put them on, he led me outside.

The blast of heat hit me like a boulder. I couldn't ever remember it being so hot, not even on the hottest Summer day. The sky was pure blue now with none of the high clouds I'd seen earlier.

"We'll take it slow," Breyard said. "I know you're not used to this."

"You mean you can get used to this?"

He chuckled. "Just like you get used to the cold in Winter. But you'll have the last laugh when we get back to the mountains and everyone else is freezing. C'mon. Let me show you around a little."

We walked—slowly—along a path of pink gravel that led from the front door of the single-story building that housed the infirmary and through the rock garden I'd seen earlier. The road turned out to be a long, thin strip of some hard, white material. Across it, shiny white sand went to the water's edge. Small waves from the dragons' play in the deeper water lapped against the shore. I stood on the road watching the red dragons. Would I ever get used to seeing so many of them?

And so much water! In the middle of the desert! One of my favorite childhood stories was about a family of mice who lived at a desert waterhole and had adventures involving other animals who stopped there for water—snakes, hawks, jackals, and even an especially funny wildcat. Most of the story, of course, involved the mice avoiding getting eaten. But I'd never imagined a lake such as this one.

"We'll stop by the shore on the way back," Breyard said. "I want you to see the market first."

I went with him, the oppressive heat making me want more than ever to dip my toes into the cool-looking water.

Soon we came to a row of houses. Made of a yellowish clay, they were only one story tall and each one seemed to spread out forever. Wide windows were open to catch any breeze that might waft by, while shades made of reeds covered the windows where the sun shone. A man came out of one house to roll up the shades along the east side of the house now that the sun had passed its zenith.

"See the towers?" Breyard pointed to the nearest roof. I saw that each house had a square tower, about one-story high, with arches open on all sides so you could see right through. Several wood poles crisscrossed the arches. "Those cool off the house."

"You're joking," I said, giving him a suspicious look. He loved pulling my leg.

"No, really. *Really*," he insisted at my continuing doubt. "They capture the breeze and direct it inside. Those wood poles—you can hang wet clothes on them to help even more. Of course, it won't get hot enough for that until Summer, they tell me."

I still wasn't convinced. Pulling practical jokes was one of Breyard's favorite pastimes, and I hated falling for them.

We turned down another path between two of the houses. By this time, my face was coated with sweat. I wiped it with the ends of the sash. How could anyone stand living in heat like this? I was just about to ask Breyard to take me back when a jumble of color assaulted my eyes. A moment later, I caught the odor of spiced meat cooking.

Back home in Barrowfield, I'd gone to market every week with Mama. And while in Penwick trying to rescue Breyard, I'd been at the capital's market. But even that one—crowded and colorful and bustling with activity—paled in comparison to this one.

Down the first aisle, bolt after bolt of thillin in every color and shade imaginable dazzled my eyes. People, all dressed in more bright clothes, haggled over prices at the tops of their voices, a disconcerting difference from the discreet way bargains were struck back home.

But I soon wearied. Breyard wanted to show me more, but I insisted. I felt shaky and weak, and all the noise rattled my nerves. We turned around and retraced our steps.

I felt only a little better when we'd left the crowded marketplace behind.

"Can we stop and rest a minute?" I asked.

Breyard looked at me anxiously. "You do look done in. Can you make it to the lake shore? It's just a little farther. I bet getting your feet wet will help."

That sounded appealing, so I nodded and kept moving.

When we got to the beach, I found the loose, white sand hard to walk in. It took much more effort to walk across than I would've expected, and the hot sand almost burned my feet when they sank into it as I walked.

At the water's edge, we took off our sandals and waded in. I stopped when the water was up to my knees, holding up my skirt to keep it from getting wet.

"Don't worry about your clothes," Breyard said, continuing walking after I stopped. "They'll dry in no time."

The water was warmer than I expected, but it still felt refreshing. I let the skirt fall and took a few more steps, then bent over to splash water on my face and head. Breyard dived under the surface and came up again far from where he'd started. I was now in up to my hips, and that was as far as I planned to go.

There weren't any more dragons out on the lake, and I wondered where they'd all gone. Hunting, perhaps? No, not in the hottest part of the afternoon. More likely sleeping, which, frankly, I was looking forward to doing myself.

Breyard disappeared underwater again, and I decided to go sit in the sand to wait for him to finish his swim. I'd taken no more than a step or two when something grabbed my legs and pulled them out from under me. With a scream, I fell backward into the water, and it closed over my head. My mouth and nose filled with water. At first I couldn't regain my footing, but the water wasn't very deep and it didn't take me long to right myself. I stood up, coughing and spluttering, to find Breyard standing there laughing.

When I could speak again, I shouted, "What was that for?"

"Aw, c'mon, Donavah, you're not still scared of the water, are you?"

Him knocking me over had been annoying and a little frightening. Laughing at me was infuriating. My being tired didn't help.

"Just shut up!" I exclaimed, brushing my hair back and wiping water from my face. "I'm going back." I started to turn, but he caught my hands in his.

"No, no. You're not getting away that easily. Come a little deeper."

"No, Breyard!" Real fear displaced my anger. "No! I don't want to!"

He pulled me a few steps despite all my attempts to resist him. The water was up to my waist now. I knew you could drown in four inches of water.

"No!" I screamed, struggling to get my hands free. "Let me go! Let me go!" Tears streamed down my face as I pulled with all my might.

"All right," he said, keeping hold of me but no longer pulling me toward the deeper water. "Donavah, I was only teasing."

"Let go! Let go!" In a dead panic now, I kept fighting him. Water splashed everywhere as I flailed around.

Breyard took a step closer to me and picked me up. Afraid he was going to take me to even deeper water, I tried to push myself out of his arms, but he was too strong for me. A moment later I realized he was carrying me back to shore.

"I'm sorry," he said, setting my feet back on dry land.

I pushed him away from me. "You know I'm afraid of the water," I said between racking sobs.

"I know, and I said I was sorry. Calm down."

"Don't you dare tell me to calm down," I shouted. "You don't know what I've … what it's like to … "

"All right, all right. Look, here are your sandals. Put them on, and I'll take you back to the infirmary."

I brushed my angry tears away and put my sandals on, then headed back without saying a word. Breyard hurried to catch up, but I ignored him.

He was right about the clothes. Despite the fact that it took only a few minutes to get back to the infirmary, they were practically dry. I went in, snatched my nightshift from my bed, and went into the cubicle to change back into it.

I stayed in there much longer than necessary, first getting

my emotions under control and then hoping Breyard would give up waiting for me and leave.

Now that fear had loosened its grip on me, I felt stupid for how I'd acted. Nothing like that had ever happened before. Breyard had been teasing me all my life. Why would I so completely lose control of myself this time? My rational mind knew that Breyard would never let me drown, so what had set me off this time?

When I finally went back to my bed, Breyard was gone. But Jinna was there, a worried expression on her face.

"I'm all right," I grumbled in response to her unasked question. "I just want to take a nap now."

She nodded. "Would you like something to drink?"

"Actually, yes, please. I would."

I bunched the blanket up at the foot of the bed and climbed in under the sheet. Jinna came back a moment later with a glass of water and a pitcher, which she set on the table.

"If you need any more—"

"Yes, I know, ring the bell." Then, after a short pause, "I'm sorry. I'm just tired."

She nodded. "I'll check on you later."

Surprisingly, I fell straight to sleep.

The time differential between Hedra and Stychs is a tricky and deceptive thing, and more than one dragon has succumbed to its wiles.

It is no great thing for the mighty red dragons to go back and forth between the worlds. A single jump or even a return trip presents no difficulties.

No, the danger lies in miscalculating the passage of time when making multiple trips.

Let us make a concrete example and say that you remain in the other world for ten years. Upon returning home, you will be ten years older, but only an instant will have passed. A disconcerting thing for your loved ones, no? Yet benign for all that.

Let us say that three years after your return home, you go back, and this time stay for five years. Beyond the obvious dubiousness of your wisdom in this matter, there are now, as you can see, two of you in the other world. This is an oddity, surely, but not a particular danger, though wiser heads than mine question what would happen if your two selves met up.

To complete the illustration, let us further say that six years after your first trip, you go back a third time. It is here wherein the danger lies, for there are now three of you in the other world, and this is too many. Only a being of immense strength and power can survive; all others will wither away and die.

Do not ask me whence comes this knowledge. It is too painful to tell.

~from the lecture notes of Tandor

Seventeen

A disturbance in the passageway outside awoke me. My head felt groggy and dull as I tried to shake off my heavy, dreamless sleep.

Botellin came into the room with an air of barely controlled urgency. He was dressed in the same clothes he'd worn earlier, but now had his red cloak on.

"Awake, I see," he said as he came to a stop at the foot of the bed. "Good. You need to get dressed and come with me immediately."

Halla walked up, a large bundle clutched to her chest. "I said she's not ready."

Botellin turned his intense gaze onto the healer. "And I say she is ready enough." He put a hand on her shoulder. "Do you not trust me?"

Their eyes dueled a moment longer, then Halla set her bundle, which turned out to be clothes, on my bed. Botellin nodded in satisfaction, then focused back on me, a fire flickering in his dark brown eyes. "Now, please change and get ready to go." He gestured to the clothes.

"Go where?" I asked, feeling stupid and slow.

"To Xyla, of course."

I couldn't move fast enough.

The clothing I changed into now was heavy and made

me sweat, but I didn't care. I was going to Xyla! And I'd need these warm things up there in the mountains. Not to mention the flight to get there.

When I got back to my bed, Jinna stood there, dressed in warm clothes and carrying two packs, one of them mine.

"You're coming, too?" I asked.

Her face fell a little. "Is that all right?"

"Of course it's all right." I gave her a smile. "I'm ready," I said to Botellin. "Let's go."

"We'll be off then," he said, then kissed Halla on both cheeks. "Thank you, my dear."

He led Jinna and me outside, and I practically had to run to keep up with his long strides.

The sight that met my eyes when we reached the front door, however, brought me to a sudden halt.

Twenty dragons or more flew overhead, each with at least one red-robed figure astride. One stood on the sand across the road, and Botellin was almost running toward him.

Kelben's voice spoke in my head. "Hurry, child. The matter is urgent."

"C'mon!" I exclaimed to Jinna, and taking her hand, I dashed to the dragon.

Botellin gave us each a hand up, Jinna first and me behind her, then launched himself as he had before. His magic made the air tingle as he sat behind me.

He held on to Jinna and me as Kelben rose skyward. The lake quickly dwindled into a blue-green jewel in the yellow landscape. Up ahead loomed the mountains.

Kelben led the way while the other dragons spread out

behind in a wedge formation, much like a flock of birds flying south for the Winter.

My breath caught in my throat. What could be so urgent that Botellin would insist on taking me from the healer's care? So urgent it required the aid of all these dragons? Was Xyla dying?

"Her life force is weak," Kelben said in reply to my musings. "She needs our strength."

The ground below began to rise, and the dragons flew higher. The terrain changed from scrubby flatland to terraced fields to sporadic woods, and finally to thick forest.

I shivered, and Botellin's arms tightened a little. Warmth spread through me.

We rose higher and higher. Before long, I saw a slash on the face of the mountainside and could even pick out the winding ribbon of the road: the bends, where Traz had fallen.

Then we soared over the pass. It wouldn't be long now.

"Xyla?" I reached out for her. Surely we were close enough for her to hear. But there was no reply.

Now that we were on the west side of the mountains, the setting sun cast its glare into our eyes. I looked down, trying to spot our destination.

Kelben began a sharp descent, and Jinna let out a cry of surprise.

"Don't worry," I shouted, hoping she'd hear me over the wind whistling past our ears. "The dragons never let us fall." I felt more than heard Botellin's chuckle.

Then there it was, the mountainside pocked with many caves. Kelben arrowed for the clearing before the largest.

We could hardly land soon enough. Kelben homed in on the clearing before the cave. He'd scarcely touched the ground when Botellin launched himself, landing as lightly as if he'd only hopped over a narrow stream. I dismounted rather less gracefully, sliding down Kelben and hitting the ground with a thud that rattled my bones. I ran for the cave, Jinna on my heels.

Botellin was right: her life vibrations were very weak indeed. The cave was warm from the heat of a large fire. Xyla looked grey. I bit my lower lip. Was she going to die? She couldn't. I wouldn't let her. I followed Botellin to her side.

Soon the other sages entered the cave. Traz ran to Xyla, his staff gripped tightly in his hand.

Botellin stood near Xyla's head, which lolled carelessly on the floor. He placed both hands on her neck and closed his eyes in concentration. The look on his face reminded me of Master Larmstro, the healer at Roylinn Academy, analyzing a patient's condition by tuning in to their vibrations.

The minutes seemed to turn to stone. No one moved. My eyes flicked back and forth between Xyla and the danse master.

Finally, the sage opened his eyes and turned to face the others. "We must strengthen her. Now. Before it's too late."

The others gathered round, their demeanor intent, their movements sure.

"What can I do?" I asked.

Botellin looked down at me, his eyes sympathetic. "Nothing for now, young lady. Stand aside and let us do our work."

"But..." I started before Botellin stopped my words by placing a hand on my shoulder.

"You do not know the magic we must do. Your own connection with Xyla will be needed before we're finished. But for now, let us do what we can."

I wanted to argue, to make him see how important this was to me, how willing I was to learn. But he'd already turned back to Xyla, so with reluctant steps I moved away. As I stood near the fire, someone walked up and stood next to me. Breyard.

"What's happening?" he asked. "What are they going to do?"

A flash of annoyance for his earlier behavior flared, then burned out just as quickly. I shrugged. "Don't know. Some kind of magic I can't do."

"Ah, right. The danse."

"I guess," I said, knowing I sounded sour and petulant.

The sages began to danse. Breyard and I watched without speaking again as the sages carried on in perfect unison. Traz had a small drum with which he kept the rhythm, and the others moved in absolute precision. Three steps to the right, a step forward, an elaborate flourish of the arms. A step to the left, two steps back, a bow, a shiver, then perfectly still for a beat, two, three, four.

I felt the gathering power that grew in strength with the danse. My feet itched to join in; my heart beat in time. It was as if someone called to me.

I closed my eyes and drew on my own maejic. Breathing deeply of the smoke-scented air, I loosed my spirit into this strange universe. It moved slowly at first, like a newborn foal taking its first halting steps. But soon it found the rhythm to soar, slipping between the clouds and the stars, whose music pierced my soul and let some of the essence of my own life vibrations mix with the ether in which I sailed. I wanted to dance across the sky, use my body to paint my signature in the bright colors of the rainbow. If I sang aloud, the notes would fall from my lips as the pure light of the moon, while the sun would join the serenade.

A spot of darkness, pulsing in the light all around, caught my attention. It felt familiar, like the touch of a dear friend. It moved away, and a sense of sadness engulfed me. I moved closer, approaching with care so as not to frighten it away. A sense of its weakness wafted to me across the ether, and I felt compelled to give it some of my strength, for I had more than enough to spare.

"Come back to me, my love," my spirit sang with its new-found music.

The darkness halted.

"Come," I sang again, and now the darkness drew near, and the light all around tinged its edges pink. "Closer still, my love."

Together, we drew back as from an unseen edge, beyond which lay death.

Then someone else's spirit approached mine. It was a gentle spirit, full of knowledge, wisdom, and merriment. Laughter flowed like water over a fall, and he guided us safely home with the power of his danse.

When my eyelids fluttered open, I was surprised to find Botellin standing in front of me, his hands on my shoulders and his lips curved into a generous smile.

"Back with us now?" he asked, his voice tender and sweet.

I nodded. "That was interesting. We shall have to experiment more another time."

Breyard looked at me with a strange, guarded expression on his face, as if something I'd done had unsettled him. I returned Botellin's smile as a wave of weariness washed over me.

"I think I'd like some tea," I said, and I was surprised at how rough my voice sounded.

Botellin nodded. "I will ask Lini to mix you up something restorative. It is one of her many specialties."

He stepped away, leaving me alone with Breyard.

"That was ... strange," he said quietly.

"Strange how?"

He shrugged. "One minute you were standing there next to me watching the sages danse, and the next you were, I don't know, sort of frozen and absent at the same time."

I'd never before thought about what happened to my body when my spirit was engaged with maejic. Now he'd got me curious. "Frozen like cold?"

"No, frozen in place. You were perfectly balanced and didn't fall over, but it felt like if I'd given you the slightest nudge, even just blew gently on you, you'd have toppled over. And even though you were breathing, it was like your mind was a million miles away. Worse than unconscious—more like dead."

I scowled. "You make it sound horrible, and it's not like that at all. It's more like being free, soaring through time and space with nothing tying you down, nothing stopping you from doing whatever you want. You'll learn." He gave me a questioning look. "When you get home. You'll learn more about maejic. But I better not say any more than that."

A few minutes later Lini came over and handed me a mug. I took it outside, hoping the chill air would help clear my head.

I'd gone only a few steps beyond the cave when laughter rang out from the woods beyond the clearing. Recognizing the voices, I stopped short. As my mind whispered his name, Grey stepped out of the trees and into the clearing. With him, as I'd known she would be, was Shandry. They were holding hands, and my heart clenched at the sight.

They froze when they saw me. It was little satisfaction to see how quickly Grey let go of Shandry's hand.

Then he took a step toward me, a smile on his face. "Donavah! You're back!"

"As you see," I said, clipping my words short. My eyes slid to Shandry, who didn't quite meet my gaze.

"But where have you been?" His eye widened as he caught sight of my cheek. "And what's happened?"

I took a deep breath. The very last thing I wanted was to start crying in front of Grey. So many things I wanted to tell him, and yet I didn't want to tell him anything at all. Especially not with Shandry standing there, a look of combined curiosity and embarrassment on her face.

I swallowed, hoping I could get out a few words safely. "I'm going to take a walk. Traz and the others are with Xyla." I walked past them.

For a short way, I followed the path, then stepped off into the trees. I didn't want anyone to find me for awhile. Too much had happened to me too quickly, and I wanted to be alone. Not totally alone in a forever sort of way, but alone on my own terms.

I hadn't gone far from the path when I came across a fallen log that seemed to beckon. I sat on it. And moped.

Grey had looked as vital and as handsome as ever, especially when he smiled. The image of him played in my mind over and over until I couldn't help but break down in tears.

It had been stupid to like him—stupid, and childish, and fanciful even to imagine he could like me back. And that was before Shandry turned up. My mind almost spat out her name. Of course he'd fall for her, with her mysterious dark skin and her beautiful eyes and her adult ways. I was just a dumb kid compared to her. And this mark on my face, that just made it all worse. Grey would think I was a freak now; so would everyone else. I wiped away my tears, only for them to be replaced with fresh ones. The dark grew deeper and my mood blacker.

✦

Now shall be unlocked a mystery, a secret thing, a hidden thing. And it is simply this: the danse is perfect spirituality wed to perfect physicality.

What is there more beautiful than the human body moving in rhythm and harmony with the spirit state? To watch is to taste and smell of the union; to danse is to partake fully, body and spirit, until one's soul is satiated.

O taste and smell. O eat and drink your fill. Join in the danse of eternity, that you may be satisfied and that your soul may grow and thrive.

~from The Esoterica of Mysteries

Eighteen

Long after my tears stopped, I still sat on the fallen log. The trees all around seemed to sense my misery, and with the new life of Spring flowing in them, they turned some of it toward me, strengthening my spirit and bringing me a crumb of comfort.

I felt someone before I heard my name called. Jinna.

My first impulse was to run away, to try to hide. But common sense took over, and I remained seated. Perhaps she would just keep following the path and pass me by entirely.

But no. Soon footsteps approached, their maker not making the least effort to hide them. A moment later, Jinna appeared, shoving her way through a tangle of underbrush.

"Oh, here you are," she said in relief. A wisp of magic wafted past as she sat next to me on the log.

I wiped my eyes, hoping she wouldn't guess I'd been crying.

"This is a nice spot," she said.

"Huh?"

"The trees here are old and wise." And somehow, though she didn't say anything about it, I knew that she knew what I'd been doing before she interrupted me ... and why.

I played along with the evasion. "Oh, right. It's a pleasant enough place to sit and think, I guess."

She nodded, then chattered on about the arrangements

being make for Xyla's care. There were many caves in the area, but only a few big enough to house dragons. Six would stay, on a rotating basis. A large number of sages, though, were settling in. If things went as Botellin hoped, Xyla would be able to fly before long, and with luck, soon after that she would be strong enough to make the transfer back to Hedra.

Somehow, Jinna's monologue soothed my raw heart and helped me get a better perspective on things.

Then she changed the subject, and I got the distinct impression that everything she'd said before was meant to lead up to this. "Actually, I'd hoped to speak with you about something."

"Yes?"

She opened a belt pouch and took something out. "I brought this for you. For when you're ready." She held out her hand on which was a thick, disc-shaped object. I picked it up and found it was a small looking glass, no bigger than the palm of my hand. I gasped. Mirrors were hard to make and therefore rare in my world.

"Oh. Um, thank you," I whispered.

Jinna stood up. "I hope it helps. Are you coming for supper?"

"I'll be along in a bit."

She gave me a satisfied smile. "Good." And she left.

When her footsteps had died away, I examined the mirror, at first trying not to see my own reflection in the process.

It was by far the finest one I'd ever seen. The glass was perfectly clear, with no flaws or bubbles in it. I couldn't even imagine what kind of material the backing was made of for the image to be so clear. Certainly something more effective than the coating of silvery paint used by most people back home.

I could see my own eyes as clearly as if I were looking into someone else's.

Finally, my glance slid to my left cheek. I examined the mark, pretending that it wasn't something carved into my own face but was an actual object of fine craftsmanship. And that much it certainly was. The lines of the knot were as uniform as if they had been made from silver wire so fine that a breath of air might break it. Coiling in perfect circles and spirals, the design had a depth that seemed almost three-dimensional.

Soola had been right: it was beautiful.

But that didn't make it any easier to accept.

I sighed, slipped the mirror into a pocket, and returned to the others.

+ + +

In the cave, Traz and Shandry were sitting near the fire tending to several pots. Grey sat nearby honing one of his knives. Botellin stood near Xyla, one hand on her flank while the other was raised into the air, palm facing upward as if to receive something from above. Breyard wasn't in the cave at all.

I walked past the fire without saying anything. Traz looked up at me, giving me a wink and a grin. I returned a small smile but carried on walking to Xyla's side.

I put a hand on her. She still felt cold—unbelievably cold, almost like stone—but her heart beat slow and strong.

Botellin's eyes opened, and when they met mine, he smiled. "You're back, youngling. Very good. I think supper is almost ready, and then it will be time for you to go to bed. You need lots of good, wholesome food and rest."

"I'm fine," I said.

He put a hand on my shoulder and steered me toward the fire. "You are strong and able to withstand much. But I have promised Halla to take care of you, or she shall have my skin."

All through the evening, the mirror seemed to burn in my pocket. Try as I might not to think of it, my mind kept returning to the memory of what it showed me.

The stew was delicious. Traz had really outdone himself, no doubt with some help from Shandry's stores of herbs and spices. An awkward silence, however, reigned at our meal. A few times, Traz tried to start up a conversation, but each attempt fell flat. I didn't want to say anything in the company of Shandry and Grey, a feeling they seemed to share. Twice I caught Grey looking at me sidelong, and both times he looked away as soon as my eye caught his. Fine. He could stare at my face some other time, preferably when I didn't know he was doing it.

After the meal, Botellin gave me two heavy blankets and insisted I get some sleep. I decided to bed down near Xyla. Wrapped in the blankets, I lay awake for a long time, thoughts and memories chasing each other in my head like cats chasing mice.

Eventually, though, I dropped off. Into a storm of dreams filled with pain, silver scars, and Rennirt's emerald eyes. I woke up in a cold sweat of terror. Voices still rumbled softly, low enough that I couldn't hear the words. If people were still talking, it couldn't be very late yet. After fitfully dozing for awhile, I fell asleep again, this time to dream of being immobile, unable to do anything for myself, able only to do another's bidding.

And so the night went, sleeping, dreaming, and waking. When morning came, I felt more tired than I had the night before.

The herb tea Botellin handed me when I got up was unfamiliar and had a bitter aftertaste. He chuckled when I made a face.

"I know, but sweetening will dilute the healing power. Drink it quickly. Faster down, sooner over."

I did as he said, shuddering as the last bit of it went down my throat. "So what's it for?" I asked, putting the cup down. I was glad that he didn't refill it.

"It will help bring some order to your thoughts." He held up a hand when I opened my mouth to object to such a suggestion. "When your thoughts are ordered, they will be easier for you to control and will not keep you up half the night." My mouth snapped shut. "I prescribe three doses per day, morning, noon, and night, until your sleep returns to normal." He smiled and raised his eyebrows at me in a questioning sort of way. I nodded in acquiescence. A good night's sleep would be welcome.

He handed me a bowl of steaming porridge. I took it with a nod of thanks and went back to my blankets to eat. From there, I watched the activity in the cave without actually participating.

Traz arose and got his breakfast from Botellin. The two of them chatted easily, Traz asking questions in an eager tone that carried to me even if the words didn't, and Botellin answering in great detail. They must be talking about danse. After a little while, Breyard joined them.

Grey and Shandry approached the fire from opposite sides

of the cave. This observation brought me little satisfaction. They ate hurriedly, then gathered their hunting gear and left.

Before long, Lini entered the cave. After she had a cup of tea with Traz, Botellin, and Breyard, she and Traz left, presumably to further his studies while they could.

Botellin cleared the breakfast things, then made two more cups of tea and came over to me, offering me one while he drank from the other.

I took the cup and sipped carefully, glad to find it was nothing more than a mild-flavored herb blend.

Botellin gestured to the floor. "Mind if I sit? I think it is time for you to tell me your story. If you are willing."

I nodded, and he sat next to me. He leaned back against the wall of the cave.

"Strictly speaking, we don't need your friends to hunt anymore. The other dragons will be able to bring food for Xyla and all of us. But I thought perhaps you'd welcome their absence, and I encouraged them to go."

Was the state of my heart so obvious, I wondered. I needed to stop dwelling on Grey and Shandry. Then my spirits rose a little, as I thought of something that hadn't occurred to me before: they didn't really have much time together anyway; once Xyla was well enough to take us home, they'd have to part company. I smiled. A truly genuine one.

"Ah, so you *can* smile," Botellin said. "How do you feel this morning?"

"Tired." How did he expect me to feel?

"As well you should. You will have time to rest, to heal, to recuperate now, while we all look after Xyla."

"And it's that simple, is it? I just sit around and after

awhile, everything will be back to the way it was?" My words and tone were bitter, and I didn't care.

Botellin sipped his tea before speaking. "No," he said, "things will not go back to the way they were. That cannot be. I do, however," and here he turned his head to look at me, "expect for you to come to terms with what has happened. I will help. We all will. But in the end, it is something you must find within yourself to do."

Tears rose to my eyes. Why couldn't, for once, someone else just make everything right again? Why did it always have to be me?

When Botellin spoke again, his voice was gentle. "Perhaps it would be easiest to start by talking about it."

The words came choppy at first, in fits and starts like a fire being made from damp wood. But Botellin turned out to be a sympathetic listener, neither interrupting with questions nor hurrying me along when I stopped to gather my thoughts.

I told him everything that had happened from the time Rennirt entered the way station until he and the other sages rescued me. Botellin made more tea when our cups ran out, and still I spoke on. At some point early in my narrative, I became aware that Xyla was listening, too.

When I finished, Botellin, speaking softly, said nothing at first beyond, "Thank you, Donavah, for your trust."

I leaned back against the cave wall, forcing myself to relax. The muscles in my back and shoulders were tied up into knots, although I hadn't noticed it until now. It was as if telling the story was like releasing a poison that had, until now, been coursing through me and that, without realizing it, I'd been resisting.

After a long while, Botellin spoke again. "Something will

have to be done now. We can no longer allow Rennirt to pursue his reckless course."

It took a moment for the meaning of these words to sink in. When they did, I sat up straight and stared for a moment at the danse master. "No longer 'allow' him?" I rose to my feet. "No longer allow him? You mean you *allowed* this to happen?" I was shouting now, and my voice echoed around the cave. "You mean you could've stopped him?"

"No!" Botellin looked up at me in surprise. "That's not—"

"If you could've stopped him and didn't, then it's your fault, too!" And with that I whirled round and rushed out of the cave, ignoring Botellin's spluttering calls of, "You don't understand," and "Please, come back."

Outside, the morning was fine, although at first I didn't notice it beyond the glad realization that I wouldn't have to go back for my cloak.

I stalked off into the trees, avoiding the main path. I didn't want to run into anyone. I just wanted to burn off this anger.

What was it with these people? Why was it so very hard to tell those who were good from those who were evil? Why did they leave evildoers free to work their harm on innocents? And why was it always me on whom the evil befell?

That made me think of Anazian. He'd been part of the mage community for years; he'd even been Yallick's own apprentice. And he turned out to be a traitor. I came to an abrupt halt. Maybe, just maybe, it wasn't as easy to tell the good from the bad as I'd always thought.

As I stood there pondering, the trees all around seemed to wrap me in their embrace.

Eventually, I walked on, my senses opening to the forest around me. The sap in the trees' veins was beginning to flow freely as the weather warmed. Small creatures moved about, some on the forest floor, some in the underbrush, and others in the branches of the trees. Insects, birds, and animals, all joining into the promise of Spring.

I walked slowly, perusing all around me—stepping carefully around shoots pushing their way up through the detritus on the ground, stopping now and again to examine an early flower, and touching the bark of the trees in greeting—until the sun was straight overhead at midday. With a sigh, I gathered my courage to go back.

I strode into the cave, just as if I hadn't stormed out of it in a tempest. Botellin caught my eye, and I steeled myself for a lecture, but he didn't say anything. In a way, that was more aggravating than if he'd lectured me, as if he were making a point that he *understood* and was behaving in an *understanding* sort of way.

The atmosphere in the cave was different from when I'd left. Several logs had been dragged in and arranged around the fire as benches. A number of sages were gathered around Xyla, and I saw that some of her color had returned. When I reached out to her mentally, all I felt was the rhythm of her sleep.

Traz was back at the fire minding the pots again. I went over to him.

"I'd have thought you'd be tired of cooking by now," I said, sitting on the nearest log.

"Nah. It's fun when it's something I don't *have* to do." He gave the last pot a stir, replaced the lid, and sat next to me. "And how are *you*, other than hungry?"

I scowled at him. "How do you know that?"

He chuckled. "As if I haven't always been able to tell."

I narrowed my eyes. "Turns out it's because of the danse, eh?"

"Could be," he shrugged. "Or maybe it's just the hungry glint you get in your eye."

Laughing, I said, "Aren't you the clever one? But you're right, as always. I'm hungry."

"Lunch will be soon."

Throughout the day, I found myself pulling out the mirror again and again, looking at how different sorts of light affected it. It flickered in the firelight of the cave and gleamed later in the bright afternoon sun.

In the evening, I handed the mirror back to Jinna, thanking her for loaning it to me.

"No," she said, folding my fingers around it. "You keep it. My great-grandfather carved the casing, and it's a family heirloom, but I think it's appropriate for you to have it. He would've approved."

"Appropriate?" I asked in confusion.

"Did you not see?"

"I saw…" I pointed at my cheek.

Jinna took the mirror and turned it over, showing me the back of the wooden casing. Carved in lines almost as delicate as those on my face was another Etosian knot.

"Thank you," I whispered hoarsely as she gathered me into a hug.

Lathan was always considered odd. When he was young, his brothers and sisters delighted in teasing him, for he was a serious child who took things much to heart. To protect himself, he took, from a very early age, to spending his time alone, hiding in the deeps of the forest, learning the ways of the trees and the woodland creatures and immersing himself in nature lore.

All on his own, though some say it was with the help of the spirits of the trees, Lathan mastered the danse.

One day, as he dansed alone, a mighty sage discovered him. Soron watched from the shadows as Lathan spun around the glade, filling himself with power.

When the danse was done, Soron stepped carefully from his hiding place, not wanting to frighten the young lad, for well he knew what could happen if one newly filled with that sort of power were to be startled. He allowed a twig to snap underfoot, then a few leaves to shuffle.

Lathan looked up at the sounds, and when their gaze met, their future was sealed.

Lathan needed no convincing to leave his life behind and go with Soron to his home far away in the mountains. And though Lathan's mother was sad for a short time that he had gone missing, greater was her relief at the removal of the burden that had been her youngest son. If any thought ill of her for not loving Lathan enough to seek him, none spoke it aloud, for all had thought him a tiresome and tedious young man.

As the years passed, Lathan learned much from Soron. Together they grew in power and might. Soron introduced Lathan to the sages at Delaron, who were impressed with the young sage's knowledge and skill.

Lathan valued his welcome amongst the sage community, grateful to be accepted there. Yet he found that he preferred the company of the great red dragons to that of the humans. He formed an especially strong attachment with Anyar.

As the years passed, Anyar often flew to Lathan and Soron in their mountain home. He would fly them back to Delaron several times a year, especially for the Summer and Winter Solstice celebrations, making it possible for them to visit the sages far more than they could otherwise have done.

But Soron was much older than Lathan, and even love cannot bind a soul to the flesh forever.

At Soron's passing, so deep was Lathan's grief that Anyar felt it from afar and sped to his friend's side.

As Soron's body burned on its pyre, Lathan performed the ritual Death Danse. Then he gathered up the remains and, borne aloft on Anyar, scattered them to the four winds.

And neither Lathan nor Anyar was seen again on Stychs.

~from the teachings of Gedden, lore master

Nineteen

As the days went by, Xyla got better little by little, improving every day, and I hoped she would soon be able to fly.

Grey and Shandry moved to her cottage a few days after I arrived. As long as they were out of sight, they were mostly out of mind. At first, my heart ached whenever I thought about them, but after awhile, I became adept at steering my thoughts into a different direction.

About a week after we arrived in the mountains, I sat in one of the other caves watching Lini teach Traz danse moves. He was a quick study—even I could tell that. And although I'd never have admitted it, not even to Traz, I liked practicing the steps myself when no one was around.

The morning's session had been particularly energetic, and when they stopped for a rest, Lini said the next part of the lesson needed to be private. I took the hint and headed back to the main cave.

The sun shone down bright and warm as I walked along. Birds called to one another, surely as glad of the arrival of Spring as I was.

As I approached, a dragon landed in the clearing before the cave. By now I'd gotten used to the easy way the sages leapt on and off the giant beasts, but something about the manner of this young man struck me as urgent. He raced into the cave shouting for Botellin. Ever sensitive to people's moods and vibrations, I instantly knew that something was wrong.

A moment later, Botellin's voice boomed. "What do you mean he's escaped?"

My heart plummeted. I hadn't quite reached the entrance to the cave yet, and I shrank back against the rock wall. Eavesdropping was bad form, but I wanted to know what was happening.

"We've searched everywhere," the messenger said. "None of the dragons could find any trace of him for miles and miles—a lot farther than he could've traveled in a week, even on horseback."

"Was not the castle watched?" Rage boiled out of the cave riding on Botellin's words. And I knew that there was only one person he could be talking about: Rennirt.

"Yes, sir. Night and day, just as you ordered."

There was a long pause during which I could picture Botellin pacing around the fire.

"Very well," he finally said, and now his voice was more like normal. "Keep up the search. Let me know if you find anything."

"Yes, sir. Any word for Halla before I return?"

"Indeed. Give her all my love." I gasped aloud at that. "And tell her Donavah is recovering even better than she could've wished."

I stayed where I was, unmoving, hoping that the messenger sage wouldn't notice me—and that the dragon wouldn't think to mention I'd been standing there listening.

The young man mounted the dragon, who immediately took off, and I watched them disappear.

Rennirt was on the loose. Free, to do whatever he wished. To track me down. Where could I hide? Was there anywhere he couldn't find me? Panic took my breath away. He could be here right now, hiding in the trees, watching me.

Of their own volition, my feet took off running straight to the only place I knew I would be safe: to Xyla's side.

Botellin, lost in thought, stared into the fire, a frown creasing his forehead. He didn't even seem to notice my arrival at first. I ran to Xyla, who lay sleeping. I leaned against her, taking deep breaths to try to calm myself.

It didn't work. The dragon opened an eye.

"What has happened, Donavah?" she asked, alarmed.

My tears flowed freely, even as I wished them away. "He's coming after me. He's going to find me." I touched my left cheek. As if the thought of him were enough, the mark began to grow warm. Or was it just my imagination?

Botellin's head jerked up and he looked over at me, then let out a groan and seemed to shrink a little. He came over to me and put his hands on my shoulders.

"You were the last one I wanted to know, and here I find you're the first."

"He's coming for me, isn't he?"

"No. No, he's not." He gave me a tiny shake to emphasize his words. "He's trying to escape my wrath."

"And he's succeeded!"

"He has, perhaps, succeeded for a time, but I shall find him, wherever he is, whatever hole he's found to hide in. It's not in his nature to stay hidden for long. It's nothing for you to worry about."

I wiped my tears away. "That's easy for you to say."

The sage nodded. "You're right, it is. And hard for you to believe. I understand." He put an arm around my shoulder and guided me to the fire. We sat side by side in silence for a few minutes.

"Donavah," Botellin finally said, "you cannot let fear rule your life. If you do, he wins. Not because of this," and he caressed my cheek with a warm hand. "This is something physical that has no power to control you. But fear . . . fear can control you all too easily."

And that was something he was right about. For many days, I didn't leave the cave much, and when I did, I didn't go far—or alone.

As Xyla grew stronger, I grew weaker—not in body, but in spirit. It was all I could do to make myself meditate twice a day, and remembering how I'd met Rennirt's spirit during that meditation session kept me from having much success.

Staying in the cave all the time meant I no longer got to watch Traz's danse lessons. I missed it a little, but he spent every afternoon showing me what he'd learned in the morning.

On the other hand, it meant I also learned things I might otherwise not have. Botellin, I discovered, met with the other sages every day. Much of the discussion was about Xyla's health, but one day, they started talking about plans for our return to Hedra.

My heart perked up at this news. Of course, the thought of returning in the midst of the dragonmasters' attack wasn't exactly pleasant, but somehow, it seemed preferable to meeting up with Rennirt again face-to-face.

And then, one day Botellin asked me to come speak with him. There was something about his air that put me on my guard, as if he had bad news.

"Well, we have come to the point," he said, and his green eyes glittered as he looked at me. The corners of his mouth twitched, as if he were holding back a smile. "The dragons have decided to return to Hedra with Xyla."

"What?" I exclaimed. "Go back with us to Hedra?"

"Come now, Donavah. You can hardly be so surprised."

Xyla spoke to me before I could utter another word. "What do you think all this was about, if not to fulfill the ancient prophecy?"

"Well, yes, but ... " No clear thought formed in my head.

Botellin grinned down at me. "Do you not want them to go with you?"

"Well, of course. But how?"

"That is the question."

When he didn't say more, I replied, "And what is the answer?"

He rose to his feet. "Come, walk with me."

I eyed the entrance to the cave. It would be nice to spend more than a few minutes out in the fresh air. Surely no harm would come to me if I were with Botellin. I stood up.

The sage smiled. "It's much too beautiful to stay inside, and I know of a wondrous place you might not have discovered yet. I want to try an experiment, if you're willing."

We took the main path, the one that led to the road. We hadn't gone far, though, when we reached a place where the undergrowth was especially thick. Botellin turned aside here. We pushed our way through the shrubs and low-hanging branches. It was hard going. Soon, sweat trickled down my face.

As we went in farther, the undergrowth began to thin a little. Botellin seemed to know exactly where he was going, although there was no discernible path that I could see.

I began to sense an unusual vibration. It was organic yet inanimate. It didn't feel threatening, but its unfamiliarity set me a little on edge. Then we stepped into a clearing, the morning sun filtering through the trees and shedding a dappled green light onto the source of the strange vibration: a stone circle.

The stones were bluish-green, uniform in size, shape, and color. They stood about six feet tall, and the upper third of each one had been carved with designs of interlocking circles and squares. They were ancient now, and the carvings had worn with age and weather, but the designs were deep, and it would take many ages yet for them to wear entirely away.

Stepping inside the circle was like falling into a cloud. Things beyond the stones looked fuzzy, and my balance faltered a little. The stones themselves seemed to be buzzing, and if I listened carefully, I could almost make out the words of a song.

I held out my arms and turned slowly in place for a moment, letting the vibrations center themselves on my soul.

"Hold a moment." Botellin's voice interrupted me.

I let my arms drop to my sides and faced him. "What experiment did you have in mind?" I asked.

"I would like to see what happens when we try to combine our powers—my danse and your maejic."

This idea surprised me. "Sounds intriguing. What do we need to do?"

Botellin gave me a shy half-smile. "I'm not entirely sure. I thought this would be a good place to try, since nature's own power is strong here, amplified and multiplied by the resonance of the stones."

I nodded. I'd experienced the resonance of stone circles before.

"As we've discussed," Botellin went on, "maejic is based on stillness and control, while danse's foundation is motion and freedom. I have grown curious to know what will happen if we work the powers in tandem."

"Oh!" I grinned at the master. What a wonderful idea! Even if nothing special happened, it would be fun to try. Suddenly, I felt as excited as I had when I was a child learning a new spell from our village magician.

"What do we need to do to begin?" I asked.

We stood for an awkward moment looking at one another. What, indeed? It was one of those things easier talked about than done. Botellin cleared his throat.

"I guess we must just do what's natural." He turned away from me, moving to the nearest stone. Then he started walking along the inside of the circle.

I concentrated on the cadence of his steps, listening to his footfalls when he was behind me and out of sight. When he came back into view, his arms had joined the danse. Without quite realizing I'd moved, I found myself in the exact center of the circle. I closed my eyes.

Power flowed and sparked in the ether and in the air. I stretched my arms out, drawing it into myself, filling my soul.

Now I could hear the song the stones sang, and Botellin's

dansing footsteps struck the counterpoint. My mind filled with swirling colors that pulsed and flashed to the beat.

Eyes still closed, I began to move. First, no more than swaying in rhythm, but soon spinning and leaping. Sometimes, my hands clasped with Botellin's, as if the danse had been long rehearsed. On those occasions, the power swelled around us to a crescendo, and I breathed it deeply.

When I opened my eyes, I found the circle filled with a rainbow. Strands of colors arced off the standing stones, weaving an intricate pattern that glowed in the sunlight shining down from directly overhead.

Botellin and I kept dansing. In perfect unison, our bodies, minds, and spirits moved in the circle and in the power. Faster and faster we dansed around and across the circle. My feet hardly seemed to touch the ground. Lighter and lighter I grew, and then I was airborne.

I flew from stone to stone, touching each as I passed, and with each touch absorbing more power until there was no substance left to my body: all was color and light.

Botellin, too, soared through the air. A moment later, we met in the center and our hands clasped, our fingers interlocked, black on white and white on black. A splash of joy welled from our souls and wrapped us in a sweet scent, sweet but not cloying, sweet in the manner of the new blossoms of Spring.

An hour or more later, I became aware that I lay sprawled on the ground. My muscles felt weary, as if pushed to do unaccustomed exercise. My soul felt refreshed and replenished. I sat up to find Botellin sitting up and leaning against one of the stones, his eyes closed and the light falling full onto his face. I cleared my throat, and he opened his eyes.

"Well," he said in a bemused tone. "Interesting effect when we combine the magics, don't you think?"

I smiled in agreement.

+ + +

A few days later, Xyla declared that the time had come for us to return to Hedra.

I gasped aloud. "What? You mean just like that?"

It was afternoon and she lay outside the cave basking in the warm Spring sunshine, while Traz, Lini, and a few other sages practiced danse moves in the clearing before us.

"I am well enough," she said. "Do you not wish to go back?"

"It's not that," I said. "It's just such a surprise."

"Tomorrow," she said with a tone of finality. "I have told Botellin."

She must have told Grey, too, or perhaps Botellin sent word, for he and Shandry arrived in the late afternoon.

Botellin gathered us together after the evening meal.

"The time for partings has come," he said. "Xyla says she is well enough to return, and I agree with her that it is not wise to tarry here longer. Now, Lini, are you sure you wish to do this thing?"

"Yes, I am sure. The good I can do here can also be done by others. The good I can do for this lad," and she grinned at Traz with obvious affection, "must, I think, be done by me. Who else would want to leave behind the life they have here?"

Her gaze met Botellin's and held for a long moment. He nodded and said, "Yes, I understand," and his voice was colored with sympathy that made me curious. Traz, on the other hand, beamed.

"So everything is settled," Botellin said. "Tomorrow we will go first to Delaron, then on to the Danse Tree, a place of mighty power. We will perform the ritual there to send you all home."

After the meeting, I went outside to enjoy the last of the sunlight. Breyard came and stood beside me.

"I suppose," he said, "it's time to say goodbye."

"I hadn't thought of that. It's strange."

He put an arm around me. "It is. Strange to think that you'll see me again before I see you. Remember, I'm proud of you."

"You're not too bad yourself," I said with an embarrassed little laugh.

+ + +

The flight to Delaron was exhilarating. We rose higher and higher into the air, and the peaks of the mountains ahead of us cut a sharp outline against the bright Spring sky. Then we were high enough to clear the pass, and the morning sun glared into our eyes. But I didn't care. I shook my head and let my hair flow behind me, glad for the chance to fly openly and freely, as we could never do back home.

When we passed over the area I thought must be Rennirt's lands, I forced myself to look down. He could do nothing to me now.

Then we were over the desert, quickly approaching the large blue gem that was Delaron Lake. Shiny specks in the sky resolved into more red dragons as we drew closer, and soon the air was full of them, above, below, and all around. The sight nearly took my breath away, and I had to wipe a tear from my eye.

The flight of dragons swooped in unison around the lake. A few peeled off with each circuit we made, landing on the wide beach of white sand on the side opposite where the town sprawled, and where a large group of red-cloaked sages had already gathered. On the last lap, only Xlya and Kelben were left, flying wingtip to wingtip.

When we finally landed, the beach was more red than white, what with the dragons and the sages. I slid off Xyla's back and looked around for the others. It was hard to spot them in the crowd.

I found Grey and Shandry near the edge of the group. He had an arm around her shoulders and was wiping tears from her cheeks. Feeling a little guilty that I didn't have much sympathy for her, I turned my gaze away.

Traz stood talking with Lini. His face suddenly lit up, and he began gesticulating wildly. I expected him to break out dancing any moment.

But when I caught sight of Breyard, my jaw fell open in surprise. He stood chatting with several sages and holding hands with Jinna. I closed my eyes, gave my head a little shake, then looked again. It wasn't a trick of the light, they were definitely holding hands. Ah, I thought, if only I weren't getting ready to leave. How fun it would be to tease him. But there wasn't any time left for that now.

I wiped away the sweat that had accumulated on my brow. My clothes were far too warm for a Spring morning in the desert, but there was no point in changing them. Soon I would be home and it would be Winter again.

Botellin looked up at Kelben, who let out a loud trumpet, making both people and dragons jump in surprise. All the sages moved forward to stand in a large group. Despite their cloaks being made of thillin, I wondered how they could stand the heat.

My attention wavered as thirst overcame me. My tongue felt as if it were swelling. Botellin began speaking, but I didn't listen to a word he said. My face grew warm, as if I had a fever, and all I could think of was drinking cool, refreshing water. I wiped my forehead again.

I began to sidle away. Surely it wouldn't hurt for me to slip over to the water and get a drink. I would only be gone for a moment. Under the hot sun, my face grew warmer.

No one, not even the dragons noticed I was moving; their attention was all focused on Botellin. His words were nothing more now than a dull rumbling in my ears. I kept moving.

At the waterside, I considered taking off my boots so I could wade a short way into the lake. But no, that would just take time, and my thirst had grown almost beyond bearing. I crouched down and scooped up a double handful of glorious, wet water.

Before I could get it to my mouth, though, a shadow fell over me. Starting in guilty surprise, I dropped the water.

"I just needed—" I started to say when something sharp pricked the side of my neck.

"Not another sound if you please. Keeping your movements invisible from the others is taxing enough without having to muffle your noise, too."

Rennirt!

✦

Karilla sat, still and silent, in the cool of the morning, eyes closed and spirit attuned to the power of the earth. Its resonance beat in time with her heart, its rhythm stirred her soul.

She knew not that she rose up, her feet spinning out the fullness of her communion with the cosmos, her body moving in time with the heartbeat of the earth.

As she swirled and twirled and leapt and spun, power unknown came to her, filling her, stirring her soul, bringing her unity with the spirit of the world.

And when she rested, she reflected on this new thing, this new source of power with which one could do great good... or great evil. She chose the good.

Thus she was the first in all of that world to danse.

~from the teachings of Gedden, lore master

Twenty

"Do not speak," Rennirt's silky voice continued, "and do not call the dragons, or I shall slit your throat."

I gave the tiniest of nods, little more, really, than raising my eyebrows.

"Stand up." I did as he instructed. One hand gripped my shoulder while the other held the knife in place. "Move."

The hand on my shoulder guided me to the left. I followed the water's edge for a quarter of an hour, not letting my mind even think lest it call Xyla or the other dragons to me. I wouldn't get any satisfaction from Rennirt's death if he killed me first—which he no doubt would.

Finally, we reached a formation of tall boulders that created a small cove with a deep, secluded beach where three very fine horses stood saddled and stamping their feet, their reins held by a guard.

Rennirt kept the knife in place. I wondered whether it was blood or sweat that trickled down my neck and into my tunic.

"Tie her hands," he instructed the guard.

With a smile of pleasure that disgusted me, the guard—a strong, lithe man whom I might have considered handsome in other circumstances—bound my wrists together.

"Put this in her mouth, and make sure she doesn't spit it out."

The guard took what Rennirt handed him, and this time I saw that it was a polished black stone the size of a small egg. The guard pried my mouth open and slid the stone in, then, as Rennirt had done before, tied a long strip of cloth around my mouth. And also as before, I felt my maejic freeze within me. There was no chance now of calling the dragons.

"Now we must ride," Rennirt said, finally taking his knife from my throat.

The two of them set me on one of the horses, tying my wrists to the pommel, adjusting the stirrups, and tying my feet to them. There would be no falling off this horse.

They mounted up. The guard took my horse's reins while Rennirt hummed a long solitary note and made a series of complicated movements with his arms.

"It would work better," he said, "if we weren't racing the wind, but it should do well enough in a pinch. Ride out."

"Yes, sir."

The guard went first, leading me, while Rennirt brought up the rear. To our left, maybe half a mile away, I could see the dragons still gathered. No one appeared to miss me yet.

Once clear of the large boulders, we galloped. I'd never ridden a beast so fine, and even with my hands able only to grip the pommel, it wasn't hard to keep my balance. At this speed, in this heat, the horses would be spent quickly; we must not be going far.

Although the desert floor had looked completely flat from the air, I now saw that it was indeed textured, with dips and rises, and with a considerable amount of plant life that managed to eke out some sort of existence. Most of the plants—

spiky cacti and other such things—grew close to the ground. But there were occasional short trees of a kind I didn't know. Everything growing had a greyish cast to it.

Now that there was nothing to do but keep my seat, I began to take notice of how uncomfortable I was in my heavy clothes. Hot and thirsty. Yet not as thirsty as I'd been before. With a sickening lurch in my stomach, I realized what had happened: Rennirt had gotten inside my head without my detecting it and had enchanted me into doing exactly what he wanted.

The quality of the air began to change. It didn't get either warmer or cooler; it was more a sense of power growing, drawing us in with thickening tendrils.

The guard slowed the horses, and now Rennirt went first. Ahead was a wide flat expanse in which stood the remaining stump of a tree. It was at least three feet in diameter, not huge as far as trees went, but much bigger than the other spindly trees I'd seen scattered here and there across the desert floor. The edges of the stump were fuzzy, as if blurred by the magic that swirled around it. My maejic might be frozen inside me, but that didn't stop me from feeling the power.

We came to a stop near the long-dead tree. Rennirt dismounted and tossed his reins to the guard.

He approached the stump slowly, his blue cloak billowing out, and held his arms straight out ahead of him, palms facing the tree and fingers outstretched. He stopped before actually touching it. His breathing changed, growing deep and loud.

I sat motionless, sweating and wishing for a breeze to dry the sweat that dripped into my eyes.

After a few minutes, Rennirt turned to face me, his emerald

eyes gleaming even in the bright sunshine. He had a satiated expression on his face, as if he'd just eaten a large meal, yet his eyes still held a greedy light as he looked at me.

"You have caused me no end of trouble, and I will now solve this problem that is you. Permanently." He nodded to the guard, who dismounted, untied my hands and feet from the saddle, and dragged me off the horse, throwing me to the ground. I put out my hands, still tied together, to break my fall, but all that did was cause all my weight to land on them. My left wrist crunched, and a searing pain shot up my arm and straight into my brain. At the same moment, my chin struck the ground, and blood filled my mouth as my tongue was caught between my teeth and the stone.

I lay there, eyes tight shut, trying to catch my breath and clear my mind of the pain that pulsed through me.

Strong hands picked me up, and the movement sent waves of agony through me. A moment later, Rennirt pressed my back to the stump. Direct contact with it sucked me into the vortex of its magic.

The ground shifted beneath my feet, and I fell upward. I sped through a purple sky, with lights of every color flashing around me.

A voice, ancient and deeply rooted as the hills, spoke.

"Why do you disturb my rest?" The words shook my very soul.

"Please, who are you?" I asked, my voice weak and unsteady.

"I am Etos, Master of the Danse. But I perceive that you are not here of your own volition."

I was no longer speeding across the sky but instead I

floated, slowly spinning in place, trying to fight off dizziness and the tightening pain that coursed through my body.

"No," I gasped.

"Then I shall refrain from slaying you. For now."

Sobs wracked my body and filled my mind with red haze. It was hard to breathe.

"But," and the voice took on a bemused tone, "you are not from this world."

Terror tore through me. Was this Etos really Rennirt, probing my mind again, and me helpless to stop him?

While I tried to bring order to my chaotic thoughts, Etos spoke on. He told of the mystical origins of the danse, of his burgeoning power that grew in strength and subtlety through the long ages, and of his ultimate assimilation into the fabric of the universe.

Surely it must be a fascinating story, but my mind was able to grasp hold of only small snippets.

Something warm trickled down my neck, and with a jolt I found myself back where I'd started.

During the time my mind had drifted in the ether with Etos, my captors had bound me tightly to the stump. My left wrist throbbed in time with my racing heartbeat.

Rennirt stood before me now, holding a crescent-shaped basin and a dagger, both made of silver. The point of the dagger was red with what I knew was with my blood. He reached for me with an elegant hand. I turned my face away, but that didn't stop him getting what he wanted. He stroked my neck, sending a shudder through my frame. When his hand came away, more of my blood coated his forefinger. This he licked off slowly, savoring the flavor with obvious relish.

Then he held the basin to my neck.

"I will have your power," he said. "I should not have bothered trying to keep you alive the first time. This way will be more efficient. And fortunately for you, bleeding to death is not painful. Just time-consuming with a cut this small."

He dipped his finger into the basin and licked up more of my blood.

"Ah, yes. Yes." He took a deep breath and let out a satisfied sigh. "You do know, do you not, that power, like life, is in the blood?" Now he reached toward my face, and his hand stroked my left cheek. I steeled myself for this new pain, but it didn't come. "It *is* too bad, though, that this bit of art shall meet a premature demise."

Something flashed in the sky in the middle distance. It must be a bird, though why a bird would be in this forsaken land I couldn't guess.

I closed my eyes, trying to ignore Rennirt's continuing caresses.

"Your blood is rich," he whispered. "Just a taste of it fills me with power. When I have bled you dry and drunk my fill, no one will ever be able to stop me."

A shadow passed overhead. Even with closed eyes, I could feel it.

Rennirt let out a gasp and moved away from me. I opened my eyes to find a dragon landing twenty paces away. Kelben! With Botellin astride!

The sage was on the ground a scarce second later.

Rennirt set the basin down at my feet, then stood to face Botellin. He seemed to swell with power—my power.

Botellin lifted a hand and shouted, "Hold, Rennirt!"

In a low, menacing voice, my captor said, "That is 'Lord Rennirt' to you, and I have had more than enough of your impertinence."

He, too, lifted a hand, and Botellin flew backward, stopped from crashing to the ground only by his collision with Kelben. My hope died. If the sage didn't have the strength to stand up to Rennirt, no one did.

Rennirt stepped back to my side, the silver dagger back in his hand and held to my throat.

"Stand back, or the girl dies."

Botellin stood in place, breathing heavily. "I would rather not kill you, Rennirt," he said, though his words sounded weak and hopeless.

Rennirt laughed. "Amusing. Very amusing. Perhaps I shall keep you as my jester. Would you like that? Living the rest of your life captive to my whim?" He laughed. "Accept the inevitable, Botellin. The time of the sages has come to an end. With this one's power, I shall rule you all. And your power shall be mine."

Botellin bowed his head, and my heart sank. Then the sound of animals squabbling came from somewhere behind me. Rennirt started, then looked to see what it might be. In that moment of inattention, Kelben leapt, a second later snatching Rennirt from my side, the tip of his tail slashing across my waist as he swept past.

Botellin raced to me. Picking up the dagger that had

fallen to the ground, he cut the cords that bound me. I slid to a sitting position, cradling my left wrist against my chest.

He slit the fabric that gagged me, and when he'd unwound it, I spit the stone onto the sand. As my maejic bloomed with full force within me, Botellin held the cloth to the cut on my neck.

Then I began to weep in earnest. The sage wrapped his free arm around me and held me tight to his side.

"My child," he said in a quiet, soothing voice. "My poor, poor child."

Other dragons began to arrive now, and the sages they brought gathered around.

All of a sudden, my left cheek flamed for a second, and then the pain was gone. A moment later, Kelben spoke.

"Rennirt is dead."

Relief flooded through me.

I wiped the tears from my cheek with my good hand. "I'm all right," I said in a soft voice, aware that the sages were all staring at me.

Botellin dabbed at my neck. "This seems to have stopped bleeding. Luckily, it's not a large cut. I only hope you didn't lose too much blood." He reached for the polished stone. "What is—argh!" He dropped it quickly, as if it had burned him.

"It's something that … that blocks your power, keeps you from using it."

"This is what he used on you before?" he asked in an astonished voice.

I nodded.

He shook his head in disgust. "I'll have it destroyed. But I fear all this will delay your departure."

"No!" I exclaimed. All I wanted now was to go home.

"My dear, surely you see that we must attend to these new injuries."

"No," I said again. "I'm strong enough to go home. Just a sprained wrist and a small cut." I didn't mention the growing ache in my mid-section where Kelben's tail had struck me.

Breyard ran up just then. "What happened?" he gasped looking down at me in horror. "Why did you leave and not tell anyone where you were going? Where—"

"Where is the girl?" A deep voice rang out, drowning out all other sound. Everyone looked around, trying to determine the source of the voice. Everyone, that is, except Botellin. With an awestruck look on his face, he stared at the stump. A net of magic spread out all around us. *"Answer me."*

It was the voice of Etos! I recognized it now. I reached up a hand to my brother, and he helped me to rise to my feet.

"I am here, Lord," I said, trying not to sound frightened.

"Come to me."

Botellin caught my eye, and I shrugged. What did Etos want me to do? The sage looked as confused as I felt.

"Come!"

Botellin gestured toward the stump, and I took the two steps needed to bring me right next to it.

"Touch me," Etos instructed.

Not knowing what else he could possibly mean, I held out my shaking right hand and placed it on the ancient wood. A thrill passed through me.

"Do not fear me," Ethos said, and now I heard his voice in my head. "No, the others do not hear what I say now," he replied in answer to my unasked question. "When we danced together in the ether, I tasted your mettle, and I approve you. Now I have tasted your blood, too."

"My blood? How?"

"It splashed my skin."

I looked down and saw that the basin in which Rennirt had been collecting my blood had indeed overturned and some of it now stained the base of the stump.

"You are hurt, else your blood could not have touched me," Etos continued. "By your leave, I shall heal you now."

"Heal me? Just like that?" I had heard of such things, of course, but mostly as a matter of legend. The power needed for that sort of thing had long gone out of the world.

"I have the power," Etos said.

A strange sensation passed through my body, like the disturbance of a lightning storm inside my skin. It started at my toes and worked its way upward, making me feel both warm and cold, weak and strong. I felt like laughing and weeping, singing and dancing, and standing quiet and still, all at the same time.

When the sensation had passed, I stood next to Etos, my hand still pressed to his skin. For Etos was the tree and the tree was Etos. And now I was completely whole again, strong, and vital, and brimming with power, power that would be more than sufficient for the task at hand.

"Take a piece of me," Etos said. "To remember."

As if I could ever forget, I thought as I broke off a piece of wood.

I turned to the crowd of watching sages and dragons, and proclaimed, "It is time to go home."

✦

What is life?

What causes sap to flow and trees to soar skyward, flowers to bloom and fruit to burst forth, green things to grow again in Spring after Winter's death?

What allows fish to thrive below water and birds to wing through the skies?

What is it that makes a heart to beat? That makes a newborn baby to cry? That makes one to fall in love with another?

What sustains life?

Air, food, and water, to be sure. Yet these things mixed together do not create new life.

There is a spark of which few have knowledge. Seek this wisdom.

-from The Esoterica of Mysteries

Twenty-one

Something in my manner convinced Botellin immediately. He looked deep into my eyes, then nodded. "As you say." He placed a hand on my head. "Go in safety and in wisdom," he said. "May our last danse together be mighty."

"What?" That surprised me. "What last danse?"

"The one we do now—the one that will send the dragons back with you."

My jaw dropped and I stared at him, speechless.

"Did you not guess?" he asked, his smile faltering a little. "Our experiment. Mixing the magics."

I nodded, still not quite following him.

"You will lend your power, won't you?" Botellin asked me.

"Well, of course. But why? I thought the dragons could transfer between the worlds at will."

"Oh, aye, they can. The timing is the problem." I frowned in confusion. Botellin continued. "When you return with Xyla, you'll go back to the instant you left your world."

I nodded. "Yes, that's what Xyla told me."

"Well, the other dragons, if they were to transfer naturally, would transfer to *this* point in time—almost two months after the time to which you return."

"So, the magic you want to work, it's to ... " My words trailed off as the enormity of what Botellin was suggesting struck me.

"To bend time and let the dragons return with you."

"But ... but what will happen if it doesn't work?"

His eyes looked deep into mine. "We must make it work."

I took a deep breath and let it out with a solemn nod. "I will join my maejic to your danse."

The danse master smiled. "I knew you would. Together, our power will make right the ancient wrong. The red dragons will return to their place of power in your world—their world."

I straightened my shoulders and stood taller. "Just tell me what to do."

"Down here, we will danse. You will, of course, ride aloft. The dragons' flight will be its own kind of danse. You need only bring your own power to bear, let it infuse our movements and resonate through the dragons. When sufficient power has been generated, Xyla will effect the transfer."

"You make it sound simple."

Botellin shook his head. "No, it is not simple. But I have tasted your power, as you have tasted mine, and I believe in my soul that we can accomplish this thing."

Traz and Lini walked up just then. Botellin took Lini's hands in his, and, without speaking aloud, they just looked into one another's eyes. Their unspoken farewells floated on the air.

Breyard put his hands on my shoulders. "Goodbye for now," he said. "Until we see one another again."

I hugged him tight. When we pulled apart for what might, for all I knew, be the last time, I spoke the words I'd never said before. "I love you."

"I love you, too," he replied, a smile lighting his face.

He boosted me up Xyla's side while Traz reached down

his staff for me to grab onto. I took my place in front. Then they helped Lini up, and she sat between Traz and Grey. We waved and shouted our final farewells, and Xyla launched herself into the air. The other dragons followed.

My heart hammered in my chest. If I didn't calm down, I wasn't going to be able to make this happen. I closed my eyes and placed my hands on Xyla's neck.

Clear my thoughts. Breathe deeply. Find my calm center. Open my inner senses. Absorb the power of the earth, the air, the life all around.

Through my link with Xyla, I began to perceive the pattern of the dragons' flight. As Botellin had said, it was like a danse. The sages dansed below, and I felt a growing surge of their power. With a quick downward glance, I saw a solid block of red cloaks in the clearing far below.

I absorbed that power, focused it in my soul, and thrust it to the heavens. It shot from me like a rainbow, sending colors swirling through the universe. I felt lighter than air as my spirit dansed amongst the stars.

I knew every dragon's name. And every sage's. I sang their names in unison with the danse, making them into a song of hope and glory.

I was barely conscious of Xyla calling, "Now!"

Daylight disappeared and everything went black. Pinpoints of light in every color filled my vision. As they streaked across the sky, my eyes could somehow follow each one. My body flashed hot and cold, cold and hot, yet it didn't hurt. At the same time, musical chords blasted through the air in a cacophony of brilliant music. I wasn't flying on a dragon; I was flying on my own!

Then, with a painful rush, the sky burst into life again.

Green lightning shot up from the ground. With a scream, Xyla swerved to avoid it. I grabbed hold of Xyla tighter, in terror of falling off.

And then I saw a wondrous sight. Several hundred red dragons descended in formation toward the ground, all spewing fire.

There were only a few more lightning bolts after that, and the dragons charged down to where the sources were on the ground. Soon, a number of dragons skimmed the treetops, chasing those below.

I barely had time to see all this, however, as Xyla wheeled round and flew straight for the cave—and her babies.

As we drew near, though, more lightning—red this time— arced toward us from the trees. With a deafening roar, Xyla's breath ignited. The lightning shot past, making the air crackle and my hair stand on end. Xyla plunged down to where the lightning had come from. All four of us riding her screamed. I was terrified she'd forgotten we were riding on her. Surely we would all slide off and fall to our deaths. The flames of her breath licked at us, though somehow it didn't burn.

A figure in a black robe stepped clear of the trees, arms raised overhead and hands pointing at the dragon bearing down on him.

I braced myself for the lighting that must come any second. But Xyla folded back her wings for that last drop. A mighty swoop and roar, and her breath ignited the dragonmaster's robe and the trees nearest to him. I didn't look down as we regained altitude, trying only to focus on keeping my balance and to force my lungs to breathe despite my whole body being paralyzed with fear.

We leveled off and circled round. Once I regained my equilibrium, I looked down. Far below, several other dragons flew over a place where flames and smoke rose into the sky. We were too high to see any real detail on the ground, and I was glad of that.

When Xyla descended again, it was at a much gentler angle. She landed in the clearing before the cave and charged in without letting us dismount. Once inside, she came to a stop and we slipped to the ground.

I dashed straight outside again, wanting to see all the dragons again with my own eyes. Yes, they were there. We had done it!

Back inside, Xyla lay in her wallow surrounded by her babies. Everything looked exactly as it had when we'd left. It was strange to think that it was only this morning by Hedra time that we'd gone, though it seemed ages ago for the three of us.

A moment later, Yallick came running into the cave, his clothes dirty and his long hair disheveled. He skidded to a halt when he saw us.

"There you are, safe." His gravelley voice sounded wonderful to me, my first clue that I'd actually missed him. "An amazing thing has happened, a wondrous and an exciting thing. Have you seen?"

"The dragons?" I asked. So many things had happened to me in what for him had been an instant; it would take some time to catch up with one another.

"Yes!" exclaimed Yallick, throwing his hands into the air in a very uncharacteristic way. "Hundreds of them! Red, fire-breathing dragons, just like the legends say." He paused and looked closely at me, as if noticing something for the first time. "You do not seem surprised," he observed.

"No," I said, and I could hear the weariness in my own voice. "There is a long story to tell, but it will have to wait a bit. Suffice to say, we've been to Stychs and brought the dragons back with us."

"Been ... to ... Stychs?" Yallick fell into a chair that was luckily not far away.

He didn't say any more while I filled the kettle from a waterskin and put it on the fire. Despite my deep weariness, I felt pleased to have finally left my teacher speechless.

When I handed him his tea, Yallick sprang to his feet. *"What has happened to you?"* he roared, startling me and making me take a step back. He took my chin in his hand, gently but firmly, and turned my face so he could better see my cheek.

I felt my face go hot with embarrassment. Taking slow steady breaths, I willed myself calm. When he released me, though fire blazed in his icy blue-green eyes, his words were calm. "I see you have much to tell."

"We do," I said softly.

Yallick cleared his throat. "All right. With the understanding that you will tell me everything later, I will tell you what has happened here." He gestured to the cave mouth, and we went outside.

"As you have probably guessed, the dragonmasters have attacked again. I am at a loss to know how they found us."

I interrupted him. "Anazian."

Yallick eyes went wide with shock, then he sighed. "Yes, of course. How did I not think of that? You are surely right."

"I wish I'd killed him," I said.

Yallick's eyebrows shot up.

"Don't look at me like that," I said. "If I had, none of this would've happened."

Yallick took one of my hands in both of his. "And neither would the red dragons be here in fulfillment of the prophecy."

"No, I suppose not," I said.

I walked over to the mouth of the cave and looked up into the sky. Dragons flew overhead in a sparse pattern. There weren't nearly as many as had come, and I wondered where the others had gone.

Xyla's voice spoke inside my head. "To the desert. They can live there in obscurity until we sort things out here."

"Sort what things out?"

She chuckled. "You do not think that the sole purpose of them coming was to save me from the dragonmasters, do you? No, little one, there is much yet to be done to reestablish us in our proper place."

More of that prophecy. I shook my head.

Yallick stood next to me and put a hand on my shoulder. "There is another reason that it is well you did not kill Anazian. Taking the life of another affects us the rest of our lives. It is not a thing to wish to be done if one can avoid it. You did well in not killing him."

"Never really had the chance," I muttered.

"Then the wishing is immaterial." He sighed. "I will not pester you to tell me your tale, though I warn you, I burn with curiosity."

I turned to him with a small smile. "I promise I won't make you wait long."

✦ ✦ ✦

Oleeda appeared before long, the relieved expression on her face when she saw Xyla and the rest of us somewhat marred by a bloody nose and swollen eye that would be black-and-blue by morning. I tended her injuries while Yallick went outside saying he didn't want us disturbed and would take the returning mages' reports out there.

That night, after we'd eaten a meal and the others had gone to bed, Yallick and I sat at the table and talked until almost dawn. I told him everything. He listened with rapt attention, starting in surprise and turning around to look at Traz's sleeping form when I got to the part about him being a sage. Yallick turned back to me, an unexpected smile lighting his face.

"This is an interesting development," he said. "Interesting indeed."

"So what happens next?" I asked with a yawn.

"For now, to bed. The arrival of the red dragons changes everything. But tomorrow is soon enough to consider how."

+ + +

A half-played game of Talisman and Queen lies before me, the jewel pieces glowing as they sit on the black velvet, embroidered with glittering silver thread. The Queen's Heart, made of ruby, gleams at the center. Ranged about are the Talismans: mine; emerald, my opponent's, sapphire.

Anazian sits across from me, absorbing energy and my concentration. His power seems to suck the very air from the room. I can scarce breathe.

The game is almost won. My heart tells me that with a single move, I will Secure the Queen's Heart. But my brain is frozen, unable to make sense of the game pieces. A wrong move, and my enemy will take all.

Anazian says, "Your move."

I want to strike him, because I already know this.

"Perhaps you should give up and go home. Yes, that would be a plan. Home, where all is not as you left it." The laughter turned brittle. "Go to your mama and papa, where you are truly needed. If it is not too late."

With a gasping start, I awake. I'm needed at home, and I must go. Now.

+ + +

Though go we to rest now,
Say not thou "defeat."
The power of ages
Again shall be meet.

Ascent from the ashes,
Descent from the stars,
The power of ages
Once more shall be ours.

A strong one will quicken
And harvest alone
The power of ages
To lead us all home.

About the Author

The first thing I remember writing was a poem celebrating my seventh birthday. I still remember the first line, but nothing can induce me to repeat it. My poetry, with few exceptions, has not improved.

I discovered that writing is something I'm good at when I was in fifth grade, and that's when I decided I wanted to be a writer when I grew up. In seventh grade, I read *The Outsiders* by S.E. Hinton, and that's when I decided I wanted to write for teenagers.

And now, I really do write for teenagers. Only thing is, I haven't grown up yet. Nor do I intend to.

Please visit my website
www.teriegarrison.com